THE MAN THEY HANGED

ROBERT J. STEELMAN

SAGEBRUSH
Large Print Westerns

First published in the United States by Doubleday

First Isis Edition
published 2019
by arrangement with
Golden West Literary Agency

The moral right of the author has been asserted

A catalogue record for this book is available
from the British Library.

ISBN 978–1–78541–685–9 (pb)

Published by
F. A. Thorpe (Publishing)
Anstey, Leicestershire

Set by Words & Graphics Ltd.
Anstey, Leicestershire
Printed and bound in Great Britain by
T. J. International Ltd., Padstow, Cornwall

This book is printed on acid-free paper

THE MAN THEY HANGED

Jay and Tuck are two drifters who happen into Mohave City as if it were any other southwest mining town. But what they discover is a place unlike any other they've seen. Not only is there no work for them, but there isn't a drop of courtesy to be had. So they leave as fast as they blew in — but not before Tuck's light fingers get the better of him, and he steals a silver knife and fork from the one old man who's shown them some kindness. Soon the pair of them are caught and sentenced to be hanged for the crime. At three in the afternoon on the Fourth of July, the deputy springs the trapdoor, and the rest is history — but not the end. For the next stranger to enter Mohave City is one Dr. Jay Carmody . . .

CHAPTER
ONE

Perched atop the high-piled ore wagon, they resembled two mountain goats. Eyes closed against the dust, rumps sore from the jagged gold-laden rubble, they tottered and swayed and clung to each other, mumbling in blind conversation as the high-wheeled wagon rumbled through the desert.

At Mohave City the washboard road snaked down the hills to a steam-powered stamp mill at the river. The town itself, gray and parched under lowering skies, lay sprinkled about the huge mill as if a careless Creator had dumped the leavings of civilization. Topped by a great golden lion on a scaffolding, it loomed paternally over the town.

On the porch of a reed-and-wattle jacal a crippled Mexican miner shifted his position on a nail keg. An accident at the Vulture mine had blinded him, but he could feel the vibration of the ironbound wheels, and raised a knobby cane in salute. Macías, the mule skinner who had given the two scarecrows a ride to Mohave City, lifted his hat. "*Don Jaime — qué tal?*"

A blacksmith looked up from pounding a red-hot shoe as they passed. At the Star Livery Stable — Feed and Grain at Good Prices — a man gazed briefly at the

1

toiling mules and went back to making entries in his ledger. The saloonkeeper at the Empire, stacking empty beer barrels to be taken downriver to Yuma on the stern-wheeler *Cocopah*, wondered whether the two scarecrows were real. The new deputy from Prescott stepped onto the warped boards before the American Eagle Barbershop. A small man, compact, he wore a wide-brimmed planter's hat and moved gracefully, like a dancer. Watching the retreating wagon with its plumed tail of dust, he stroked the carefully trimmed mustache.

"Those two," he said.

The barber ceased trimming wiry nose hairs. "Eh?" he asked, cupping an ear against the clamor of the stamp mill.

The deputy cocked a thumb. "On Macías' wagon. See them?"

Shuffling to the grimy window, the barber rubbed with a striped towel. "Couple of drifters, I guess."

On a knoll above the mill, free of noise and dust, sat the white-columned house of the owner of the Salvador mine, the Poland, the Big Bug, the General Kautz, the Vulture, and the mill on the river. The dwelling lay in a wreath of green lawn, a verdant green maintained by water wagons from the Colorado. Flora Lamon, emerging pink and fair from the copper bath bought in Florence, Italy, was startled by her father's abrupt exclamation. Quickly she stepped into her *peignoir*, as she had learned to call it in Boston.

"What is it, Father?" she asked, going into the adjoining room.

2

In the second-floor library, Andrew Lamon bent over the tripod-mounted brass telescope he used to keep an eye on his domain: the mill, the docks, Mex Town, hoisting houses, and engine shacks scattered about the nearby hills. A black brow curled over the eyepiece; big hands were knotted together under the long tails of the coat he wore even in a blistering Arizona Territory summer.

"You cried out, I thought."

Carefully her father adjusted the focus. "They're getting down by old Major Iredale's place."

Narrowing gray eyes so that the long lashes shielded them from the glare, Flora looked out the window. "And who are *they*, pray tell?"

"Two loafers have cadged a ride on one of my wagons! I've given strict instructions —"

"Let me see!" Flora begged, anxious for excitement. After school in Boston she found Mohave City a stifling and unrewarding anticlimax, though as a small girl she had delighted to ride the ore wagons, learning Spanish from the Mexicans. Flora had sneaked into forbidden mine shafts, with Mexican boys fished for crappies in the muddy river, and dared to smoke cigarillos they rolled for her.

"Young lady!" Andrew Lamon fumed. "You had better —"

"My Lord!" she giggled. "They look like two fugitives from a cornfield! They're shaking themselves like dogs, and the dust is coming off as if it were flour! Who can they *be*?"

3

He slapped her hard on the bottom. Through the French-silk robe it stung.

"You're disgraceful! A strumpet, like your mother! Get back in there and put on some decent clothes!"

"But I only wanted —"

"I don't give a damn what you wanted, girl! Is that what they taught you at Miss Phipps' — to parade around in a scrap of nothing, like a wanton?"

She drew herself proudly up, tossing the mane of hair the color of ripe wheat, pulling the lacy robe tightly about her body. Chin high, she walked back into her bedroom, queenly and defiant. Slamming the door, she scolded her Mexican maid Luz, and wept.

Old Major Iredale, still in Confederate gray, rose as the two travelers paused before the cottage he shared with his schoolteacher daughter.

"Mister," the round little man said, tipping an ancient bowler hat, "could we have a dipperful from that well?"

The younger man, pale and lanky, with long and straggling blond hair under a straw hat, added, "We're real parched, sir. That ride on the wagon dried us out for fair!"

When the erect military figure did not move, the young man shifted his blanket roll uncomfortably. His companion, the small fat man, shrugged, picked up the carpetbag. They were about to walk on when the gray-clad veteran spoke.

"You're Sheridan's scouts, then: I know you!"

Jay took off his hat and walked up the graveled path lined with whitewashed rocks. Under the fringing cottonwoods it was cool.

"Sir," he said, "we —"

"I know Sheridan's rascals," the old man repeated. Ramrod stiff, he emerged from the vine-covered porch. "Saw enough of the devils to spot one a mile away! Rode well, they did, but Jo Shelby's cavalry were *gentlemen*, not like those Yankee rascals!"

"Yes, sir, but that was a long time ago. Now we've got one country, one president."

The old man sighed, sat heavily in the splint-bottomed chair. "Grant! That damned butcher! At the Wilderness —" He broke off, staring at nothing.

Jay crooked a finger at his companion. Sniffing about like a hound, the round little man shuffled up the walk. "He's crazy, ain't he?"

"Who's he?" the old soldier asked. "He looks familiar."

Jay ignored the question. "That's a nice-looking pitcher there," he observed. "Cut glass, too! My grandma back in Colum — I mean Natchez — my grandma back in Natchez had one just like it, with grapes and stuff cut in."

"Natchez, eh?" The faded blue eyes searched his. "Well, sir! Do you remember the old Windham place, sat on a hill out by the Baptist Seminary? Bessie Windham was my cousin. Perhaps you heard of her? Beautiful woman — played the harp. Her fingers were real short, and her mother thought playing the harp would —"

"I — I left there as a child," Jay stammered. In fact, he had been born on South Third Street in Columbus, Ohio, where all the Germans lived. Only later had they

5

moved to the hard-scrabble farm near Delaware, some thirty miles north. For the first time he noticed the tarnished oak leaves on the old man's collar. "Major," he said, "I sure could use some of that liquid, whatever it is."

Picking up the pitcher, the major poured him a glass. "Forgetting my manners, men! I'm Major Sylvanus Iredale, CSA. Have some cold tea! I always put a little Bourbon in it to liven it up, though my daughter don't know. Hard to get good whisky out here in Hell's backyard! Tell your orderly he'll find a tin cup in the kitchen."

Petulant, Tuck rose. "Orderly?"

"Cookies on the platter, too," the old man went on. "Sarah always sets out a bite for me before she leaves in the morning."

Jay bit delicately at a raisin-studded cookie. He had eaten little for two days, but restrained himself. He would have to watch Tuck, whom he could hear bumbling about in the lean-to kitchen.

"Sarah's my daughter." Major Iredale waved his cane at the small building atop the pile of tailings behind the cottage. "Mine people hired her to teach school up there. Sarah gets along famously with her children, though she gets lonely for home sometimes." He sighed again. "Like I do, I suppose. The green hills of Virginia. Well —" He broke off again.

"I had a bit of schooling," Jay remarked, "though I was never what you'd call a scholar. I studied to be a pharmacist, too. Then when my folks passed away and we lost the farm I struck out for the West. Wasn't anything to hold me in Colum — I mean, in Natchez."

Tuck emerged from the kitchen with a jelly glass, looking pleased. He took a handful of cookies to munch with his tea and sat down.

"Well," Jay said after another cookie, "we thank you for your hospitality, sir. Now we must go. My friend and I are looking for a job of work hereabouts. We're down on our luck and have got to come into funds right quick."

Tuck protested, looking at the silver glow in the clouded western sky. "Sun's dropping and we ain't got a place to sleep! Jay, maybe this gentleman would —"

"No," Jay said quickly. "We've presumed enough." He shook hands with the major.

Tuck shrugged, slipped a handful of cookies into a ragged pocket. The old man waved his cane as they trudged down the road, ankle-deep in gray dust.

"Look out for pickets! This is unfriendly country!"

At the lion-topped mill Tuck held back, putting fingers in his ears. "Damn — what a racket! *I* ain't going in there! The noise'd drive a man crazy!"

"All right," Jay said crossly, "but it's the most likely place to find work! You go across the street to the Empire, then, and see if they need a swamper. We've got to find something!"

The mill was a wooden structure straggling halfway up the hills along the river. Wagons dumped loads of ore into giant crushers powered by steam from coal-fired boilers. Smaller stamps broke the ore into finer fragments. Mixed with water pumped from the river, the slurry washed through wire screens and passed over wide oscillating belts. From there the wet gravel went into great stinking pans fired from below. It was like a scene from Dante: noise, steam and smoke, blazing fires, evil smells, hordes of half-naked Mexican workers running about, sweating and calling out to each other.

"What in hell do *you* want?" A burly red-bearded man with hot blue eyes confronted Jay. Incongruous in Gehenna, he wore a high paper collar and cravat; his white linen suit was wrinkled and damp with sweat.

"I said — what in hell are you doing in here? Didn't you read the sign? Or can't you read?"

"I can read, all right, but I didn't see any sign."

"It says NO TRESPASSING! This is the Lamon works."

"All I wanted was to find if you needed an extra hand! I can shovel ore into the crusher up there, or do bookkeeping, or whatever you need. I know a little chemistry and —"

The redheaded man gave a short hard laugh. "You don't look like a greaser to me!"

"My name is —"

"I don't give a tinker's dam what your name is, fellow! All we hire is Mexicans." The foreman or whatever he was gave Jay a shove. "Get out of my mill, quick! We don't want outsiders in here!"

Standing on the narrow wooden platform along the bubbling pans, Jay almost lost his balance. "Now wait just a minute!" he protested.

"Go on — get out! If you know what's good for you, keep going down that road till you get clear of Andrew Lamon property!"

Jay was a mild-mannered person, resigned to whatever fate brought. "I was just looking for work! It isn't any crime!" He had lost his straw hat, and knelt to pick it up. Emerging into the gray day he could feel the hot blue eyes boring into his back, sharp as an auger.

Tuck, rumpled and angry, was trying to stuff the tail of the once-expensive silk shirt into his pants. He moved hastily aside as another high-wheeled wagon, golden lion painted on its side, rumbled down the street.

"Ugly cuss!"

"Who!"

Tuck jerked his head toward the Empire. "Saloon man! Threw me out on my butt. Didn't need no swamper, and wouldn't hire a tramp if he did! Oh, he talked awful mean!" A dog slunk up to Tuck, and he kicked at it. "Get away, you!" Lifting rubbery lips over yellowed teeth, the cur limped away. "Damn if even the dog hasn't got better manners than that saloon man!"

"Or the foreman at the mill. I didn't do any good there, either, and almost got boiled in that amalgamating soup!"

At the Star Livery Stable the proprietor looked up from his ledger. "No, I *don't* need no help! Anyway, I don't hire any drifter that comes in out of nowhere. Mr. Andrew Lamon takes care of finding me help — if I need any, that is, which I surely don't."

9

At the American Eagle Barbershop they paused momentarily. The man with neatly trimmed black mustaches and a star pinned to his well-tailored vest looked thoughtfully at them. Wary, Tuck pulled Jay's sleeve. "Ain't likely to need help there, anyways!"

With no more success they tried the blacksmith shop. The oak-solid smith only shook his head and went back to banging on the iron link he was forging.

"But isn't there *anyplace* in this town a man can get work?" Jay asked helplessly. "There must be something! We're not loafers — we want to earn our keep!"

The hammer clanged on the iron, now cooling to a delicate pink. Finally the man rested the head of his hammer on the anvil to wipe away beads of sweat on his broad forehead. The shop was quiet except for the distant clamor of the mill. "Where you from?"

"Lots of places."

"You ain't ever heard of Mohave City?"

"Not till the driver of the ore wagon said he was headed this way."

"I seen you two come in the wagon with Macías. Someone'll wool daylight out of him for breakin' the rules."

"Just because he was kind enough to give us a ride from up in the hills? We'd been walking for two days!"

Wiping palms on his leather apron, the smith stuck the link back in the glowing coals. "'Twasn't a kindness," he muttered, and spoke to the Mexican boy squatting at the end of the long wooden pole powering the bellows. "Pump, *muchacho*!"

They tried the Climax Store (Coal Oil, Beans, Flour, Lard, Millinery, Axes, and Shovels, U.S. Post Office) without success. Weary, they were reduced to a Chinese eating house, the docks where the stern-wheeler *Cocopah* was unloading, and a mud-brick Mexican *cantina* where vacant-eyed Mexicans only stared at them, refusing to comprehend Jay's passable Spanish.

Finally, dejected, the pair stood again in the dusty road at the edge of town, where an evil-smelling Mexican *barrio* straggled along the swampy bottomlands. Behind them, Mohave City was shrouded in dust. Even the barren hills were gray, studded with gray bushes, their folds and convolutions dismal. Though it was early evening and the July day dying, no light glimmered on in the town. The gray people, Jay thought, were used to a drab view of life. Only the big white house on the hill showed any color. The grass was billiard-table green, and through a tall window a lamp burned yellow.

Tuck sighed, dug the broken toe of his boot in the dust. "What the hell do we do now, tell me that!"

They sat in a copse of reeds before a smoky fire, the swindler and the almost-pharmacist. A skinned rabbit cooked on a twig over a blaze of mesquite twigs. They had clubbed it to death, not savoring its struggles but determined to eat meat.

"That jack's bound to be tougher'n mule hide," Tuck observed, "but it's something solid to put into our stomachs."

Shivering in the damp night air, Jay blew a mournful chord on his mouth harp. "Never knew it could be so cold and clammy after a hot day."

Tuck poked the rabbit. "It's the river." Squatting on his heels, he grumbled. "Can't you play nothing cheerful on that thing? Here it is almost the Glorious Fourth! There ought to be bands tuning up and fireworks getting ready and beer barrels icing. Strike up a lively tune — 'The Drunken Fiddler' or something like!"

Jay shook his head, slid the mouth harp into a pocket of his jeans. "Can't seem to put my heart into it, not tonight." He looked up at a crescent of moon 'in the sea of silver-edged clouds. "Almost wish I was back on the farm again. Adventure is all right, but good eating beats anything. At least on the farm there was always enough to eat, even if there wasn't ready cash."

Tuck twisted a hind leg of the roasting animal. "Well," he said, "Br'er Rabbit's done enough for *this* child." He pulled out the green-twig spit. Fumbling in his coat, he took out a long knife and fork that gleamed in the moon's rays. Across the river a coyote, probably smelling the meat, yipped a crescendo of short barks.

"An ugly town," Jay mused.

"What?"

"Mohave City. A sick town. We're better off shut of it, Tuck. We'll hightail back down the river to Yuma, and —" He broke off suddenly. "Where in hell did you get those?"

Tuck, chewing on a stringy hind leg, stared. "What?"

12

Jay pointed an accusing finger at the heavy silver carving knife and fork stuck into the damp earth.

Tuck spat out a fragment of bone. "Where you think? That crazy old man!"

Remembering, Jay scowled. "You went into the major's kitchen to get a cup, and *stole* them!"

"Sure did!" Tuck waved the rest of the rabbit at Jay. "Try the other leg! It's a mite raw but a little blood never hurt no one. You told me once, there was tribes in Africa that drunk cow's blood and stayed real healthy."

"You stole those things right out of that old man's house!"

Tuck threw away the gnawed bone and picked up the carving knife. "Hell, yes, I stole it! We ain't never going to see the old fool again anyway!" Appraisingly, he hefted the knife. "That's solid silver, my boy! Mexicans melt it down and make necklaces and earrings and them shell things — *conchos* — out of silver. These'll bring a good price!"

Jay snatched the knife, picked up the fork. "Aside from returning evil to that old man for the good he did us — the only soul in that whole evil town with a heart in his bosom instead of a chunk of high-grade ore — you steal something that mean-looking deputy at the barbershop will come looking for! Put out the fire! They can see us for miles!"

Tuck snarled. "Give me back my knife and fork! Nobody'll miss them till we're long gone down the river!"

Holding the carving set, Jay looked toward the town. "I'm not so sure," he said. Above the high reeds scattered torches bobbed; they were coming fast. He heard a hound whoop, and the thud of hoofs on the road.

"I'm not so sure," he repeated, and waited. He was too tired, too hungry, to run.

The citizens of Mohave City gathered in a weather-beaten clapboard structure leaning crazily from long exposure to sand-laden winds. The presiding judge was the redheaded superintendent of the mill; there was a scanty jury of six. Jay recognized the barber, the saloonkeeper, the blacksmith, the man at the Star Livery Stable, and the Levantine-looking proprietor of the Climax Store. There was also a worker from the docks wearing a battered nautical cap. As witness for the prosecution old Major Iredale attended. On his arm was a plain-featured girl who must be the daughter Sarah, the schoolteacher.

"Right there, you two," the deputy ordered, indicating a wooden bench near the low dais on which the judge sat at a table.

Wind curled around the building with a low sigh. From time to time there came a rattle of sand against the closed windows. The judge wasted no time. "State your full names, you two!"

Tuck glowered at the judge. "Don't have to! You ain't got no right to try us in this kangaroo court anyway. Where's our counsel?"

Though his manner was now composed, the judge's eyes had the same intensity Jay had quailed before in the afternoon, a hard blue glow like a laboratory

14

blowpipe Jay remembered from his pharmacy apprenticeship. Jay noticed he wore a fresh white linen suit. A handsome handwoven Colombian straw hat lay on the table beside an inkwell.

"Your names don't matter," the redheaded judge said. "You're two thieves, two ne'er-do-wells, and you'll get your just deserts regardless. Major Iredale?"

Now with medals on his uniform, the old man stood up, propped by the walking stick. "Yes, sir."

The judge held up the silver carving knife and fork. "You recognize these, Major?"

"Yes, sir — I do."

"Are they your property?"

"They are. They were given to me by the members of my regiment on the occasion of their mustering out in June — no, it must have been July — anyway —"

"Were they found to be missing after these two rascals visited your home?"

The plain girl whispered to her father. Her face was pale, and the dun-colored hair drawn tightly back on the nape of her neck.

"Miss Sarah, I must ask you to stop prompting the witness!" The judge had no gavel, but tapped orange-furred knuckles on the table. "It is Major Iredale's story we want, ma'am, not yours."

A flush brought color to the pale cheeks. She lowered her head, fingers working at her reticule.

"They took them, all right," Major Iredale agreed. "There's no doubt of that. Anyway, the older one" — he pointed his cane at Tuck — "that one went out into the kitchen to fetch a cup and probably saw my carving

15

set. It's silver, very valuable, and was given to me by the members of my regiment when —"

"Thank you," the judge said. "You may sit down."

The major remained standing. Annoyed, the judge asked, "Now what?"

When the old man could not seem to find the words, Sarah Iredale rose. She appeared frightened and nervous. "We've got the silver back so we don't care to prosecute these two men. After all, they're poor and unlucky — all you have to do is look at them to see that." She looked at Jay. "I think they're sorry. They ought to be let go if they promise to stay out of Mohave City. That's what Papa and I think."

Major Iredale cleared his throat. "That's right. My daughter and I don't believe in —"

The deputy took the major's arm and drew him down into his seat. Sarah Iredale remained standing.

"Ma'am," the judge said, "you have no status in this court. Please sit down!"

"But —"

"This ain't no proper court!" Tuck shouted. "I appreciate the words that nice young lady says in our defense, but where the hell is our lawyer? The Constitution of the U.S.A., says we're entitled to a lawyer!"

Leaning back in his chair, the judge crossed booted legs. "A lawyer for proven criminals would have to be paid for by county funds. Everybody here agrees it would be a waste of taxpayers' money. You did take the carving set, didn't you?"

Jay, resigned, put a hand on Tuck's ragged sleeve. "Might as well 'fess up."

"Don't admit nothing!" Tuck bawled. "Damn it all, Jay, I told you —"

"Don't do any good, Tuck." Jay raised troubled blue eyes to the court. "You found the stuff on us, and I guess I'm an accomplice, to put the legal word on it. So go ahead and send us back to your jail. At least we'll have something to eat and a place to sleep, out of the damp."

The judge shook his head. "Not so fast, young man! This is a court of law. We've got a jury here, and it's up to them to have the final say." He turned to the group sitting expectantly in the close-grouped chairs. "How does the jury say, Monk?"

The foreman was the man from the Empire Saloon. He rose, scratching his buttocks and looking judicial. Someone in the back of the room giggled, and the judge turned a somber face on him.

"Monk?"

"They're guilty as hell," the saloonkeeper announced. He turned to his companions. "Ain't they, now, fellers?"

"Guilty as charged," the judge announced. Except for the groping of the wind against the walls and the distant clamor of the stamp mill, the room was silent. Someone laughed again, but it was quickly bitten off. "Stand up, both of you."

Grudgingly Tuck rose. Jay followed him.

"I sentence you both," the judge said, "to be hanged by the neck until dead, on tomorrow, the Fourth of

July, at three in the afternoon, in this year of our Lord eighteen hundred and seventy-eight." He banged his knuckles on the table.

CHAPTER
TWO

They had first met on the El Paso Wagon Road, alighting at Tucson with what seemed ample funds. Jay was a bookkeeper in an Indianapolis brewery, and decided he wanted to see the West. Tucker Stiles was a small-time swindler and card sharp. Jay was impressed by Tuck's worldliness, though after a time he concluded much of it was simply filling for balloons. Tuck was, like Mr. Micawber in a Dickens novel Jay had read, always sure something was about to turn up. Jay was an amiable companion, and had education, which Tuck lacked but admired in others. Too, Jay had almost been a pharmacist, to Tuck an exalted profession. Jay knew all about such things as jalap, ipecac, nux vomica, and the deadly nightshade; in his apprenticeship he had even done minor surgery, and some embalming. But the death of his folks, within three months of each other, had ended his studies a year short of the coveted certificate, and he had been forced to go to work to pay off family debts.

It did not take long to exhaust their funds. Neither could understand where the money had gone. Jay had spent money lavishly on a *muchacha* named María Teresa Lupita something something — he could never remember the string of names. Tuck, their resources dwindling, fashioned a complicated variation of the old "pigeon-drop" swindle on a promising victim. But María Teresa Lupita something something turned out to have a husband with a shotgun. On the same night Tuck's victim called the city police. Quickly they departed Tucson on the stage to Yuma, paying their fare with the small funds remaining.

Ragged and down on their luck, they cadged meals and begged rides on freight wagons along the Río Gila. There were towns and villages and rude settlements named Belcher's Ranch, Texas Hill, Mission Camp. But a rumor of new gold diggings up the river in Castle Dome City, Three Point Bend, Mineral City, and La Paz, drew them northward. With only a few coins in their pockets, a bedroll for Jay and a carpetbag for Tuck, they rode on the ore wagon into Mohave City. The day was fateful.

Windows deep set with iron bars, the jail was a structure of mud bricks between River Street and the muddy course of the Colorado. A dusty plain separated the street and river, with a rickety bandstand in the middle. Down the river, in a marshy swale, lay the huts of Mex Town. Jay stood at the window, hands clenched on the iron bars, to watch a man draping red, white, and blue bunting on the bandshell. The gray anonymity of yesterday had dissipated. Morning sun shone hard and hot on the plain. From somewhere came the tootling of a fife and the thud of a bass drum.

"Guess they're planning some kind of celebration for tomorrow," he muttered.

Tuck, lying on a string cot, wiped his several chins. "No celebration for us, and that's a fact!"

Jay watched a party of workmen carrying lumber across a field and laying it in a pile. "They can't be serious, of course — about us, I mean!"

Groaning and holding his back, Tuck sat up. "Course not! Who ever heard of people being hanged for stealing a knife and fork? Worst that could happen is a tar-and-feather job, but that ain't so bad. Happened to me once, in Danville, Kentucky. I had the devil's own time scraping that stuff off, especially around my privates. But the worst part was the rail they rid me out of town on!" Reflectively he rubbed his groin. "Put a crimp in me for six, seven weeks." Rising, he went to the barred door and yelled. "Hey, out there! Ain't it breakfast time?"

Back against the wall, slumping on a stool, Jay took out his mouth harp. Closing his eyes, he blew softly into it — "Dreaming Sad and Lonely." There had been a girl in Indianapolis who liked for him to play that old Reb song. Tuck, elbows on the deep embrasure of the window, gazed out onto the plain. "What the hell are they building out there, anyway?"

The Indianapolis girl had been slender, with milky-white skin and a rose in the high-piled dark hair. *Dreaming sad and lonely, thinking, dear, of you; dreaming sad and lonely, my heart is ever true.* It was a sad tune, in a minor key, and — what was her name? Kitty. She cried when Jay said he was going out West.

Tuck rattled the door. "Hey, ain't no one home? Bring us some grub!" To Jay he grumbled, "Ain't there no happy songs you know, for Christ's sake?"

"I'm just not happy, Tuck. Jailed for a common thief!"

"You didn't steal the stuff anyway! I did it!"

Jay knocked spittle from the mouth harp. "Well, I'm in jail, it appears to me! Besides, it doesn't make any difference who did it. They just wanted to make an example of both of us."

From time to time they heard voices, scuffling of chairs, a laugh from the deputy's office, which faced the street. No one answered their pleas for food. The furnishings of the cell were a pail of water and a dipper — river water, with silt in the bottom — and a slop jar, along with the string cots and a single stool. Westering sun finally slanted through the barred window. There was only the barred pattern on the dirt floor, the heat, the distant thunder of the mill, and a small lizard that ran down the wall and looked at them upside down. It had intense black beads for eyes, and a pulsating throat. They sweltered and waited, kept on sweltering and waiting. Finally Jay went to the window. The afternoon had passed. Quickly the hills lost their outlines and became only a purple-shrouded bulk. He started when the cell door rattled and a key turned in the lock.

Into the room stepped the neatly dressed deputy, carrying a lighted kerosene lamp which he hung on a wall bracket. Gravely he stood contemplating them, light from the lamp casting his black shadow on the floor. "And how do you find our weather here,

22

gentlemen? Warm during the day, I grant you, but at night the river cools things off. If you need blankets —"

Jay started to speak but Tuck cut him off. "What we need, and what we're entitled to by rights, is a lawyer! Who do you think you are, anyway, you people here — playing around with two U.S. citizens like they was checkers on a board?"

The deputy smiled, fingered his mustache. "Right is what people call right, isn't that so? Mohave City is a kind of city-state, like the old Greeks had. Nobody bothers us, we don't bother anybody. So that's an end to that"

Jay felt a chill wash his empty stomach. "Do you intend to starve us to death, then? Is that what the old Greeks would have done? We haven't had a mouthful of decent food for days!"

"We aren't savages, if that's what you mean. No, we feed prisoners well." The deputy raised his voice. "Polonius!"

From down the corridor a voice quavered. "Yes, sir."

"Food arrived yet?"

"Just brought it from our house, Mr. Wagstaff."

"Well, then, hurry it up! I've got an important meeting tonight!"

Bearing a tray, an elderly man wearing a Union forage cap entered the cell, back bent as if from long hoeing or shoveling. He set the tray on the stool and pulled off the cloth.

"Steak!" Tuck marveled. "And gravy!" He held up a crusty brown loaf. "Bread to sop, and pie!" Lifting the steaming pot, he stuck his nose into the exhaled vapors.

"God damn me — coffee, real coffee! I ain't had no decent coffee since Yuma!"

Jay took a chunk of steak on his fork. Perversely, Tuck began with pie, parting it in half with eager fingers and washing it down with gulps of coffee.

"There are cigars, too, on the tray," the deputy pointed out. "Picked them myself, at the Climax. I'm fond of a good smoke. I hope you gentlemen enjoy yours."

Tuck continued to wolf the pie. Jay was suspicious. "Cigars?"

"Customary. Last supper." The deputy drew out a handsome gold watch and looked at it, then motioned the old man to precede him from the cell.

"Wait a minute," Jay protested, rising.

"Yes?"

"How long are you going to carry on this farce? I mean —"

"Well, it's hardly a joke." There was almost sadness in the deputy's voice.

"Don't argue," Tuck grunted, fingers sticky with dried-apple juice; little of the pie remained. "Let them have their fun, Jay. We're the goats, but at least we get a decent meal out of it."

Jay's mother had never allowed profanity in her house, and he was pressed for words. Finally he said, "Christ Jesus — this is cruel! What kind of people are you, anyway?"

"We believe in order, that's the kind of people we are here. When that order is threatened, by whomever, we have to take steps to maintain the normal course of

24

things. Mr. Lamon's mines are very dependent on the maintaining of order."

"But —"

The door came to with a harsh click. "Enjoy your meal," the deputy said, raising his broad-brimmed hat in salute. "I'll see you both tomorrow afternoon, at precisely three o'clock."

Jay paced the floor. "Tuck, this is crazy! It's something out of a book — a novel, like some of the scary things Edgar Allan Poe wrote!"

Tuck slipped a remnant of steak between two slabs of bread, poured the rest of the gravy over the combination. "I ain't ever read many books like you have. Did know a man named Poe once, though. Willis Poe, used to tailor suits for me back East — when I was in funds, that is."

"Don't you understand? They're really planning to hang us, tomorrow at three!" Desperate, he pulled Tuck's hand away from his mouth. "Stop eating and listen to me! There's no law in Mohave City except what they make it! God damn it, we're in danger!"

Stolidly chewing, Tuck finished the meat and bread. "Listen, Jay — don't get panicky! Tomorrow's the Fourth of July, remember? Lamon or whoever owns this burg is probably giving a picnic with free beer to the townsfolk, specially those poor Mexican bastards that work the mines. You and me — we're just part of the celebration, like fireworks. They'll josh us a lot, maybe put us in stocks and throw rotten vegetables or horse apples or tar-and-feather us, like I said, but hell! Even if this is Arizona Territory it's still part of the

U.S., ain't it? They can't hang a man for just picking up a silver knife and fork!"

Frustrated, Jay sat down, gnawed at his knuckles.

"It ain't likely to be beer and skittles tomorrow but we'll live through it! We'll take her just as she comes, pardner!" Going to the door, Tuck rattled the bars fiercely. "Hey, out there!"

Carrying a lantern, the old man shuffled down the hall in carpet slippers.

"Bring us a couple blankets, Felonious or whatever your name is! We're guests of the city, and have got to be treated with respect! While you're at it, see if you can get them to stop that hammering and sawing down by the river! A man needs his sleep!"

"That man is evil," Jay muttered.

"Eh?" Wiping fingers on his shirt, Tuck looked up. There was little left of the meal, but Jay had lost his appetite anyway. "Who?"

"The deputy."

"All he is is Lamon's tool. You talk like he was a spook!"

"He is."

Belching, Tuck lay down on a cot and rolled a blanket about him. Jay remained at the window, listening to the clamor along the river, watching the glow of torches. At last he sat down on the other cot, listlessly picked up a blanket. Tuck snored, mouth open and hands crossed on his belly. Jay shook his head. Tuck just didn't realize what they were up against. As long as his belly was full, he never worried about anything.

26

Finally he dozed, and woke only after a bad dream. Wild-eyed and trembling, his heart beating like a Gatling gun, he sat up on the cot. There was no sound; everything was quiet. The jail slept, Mohave City slept, the workers along the river had gone to bed. Tuck slept, snoring; Jay's nightmare had not stirred him. Jay sighed, lay down, and pulled the burr-studded blanket about him. He slept again, almost, when he heard a voice.

"Are — are anyone?"

Sitting abruptly up, he listened. The sound had seemed to come from the barred window.

"Hallo, inside! *Señores?*"

Earthen floor damp under his bare feet, Jay hurried to the window. "Who's there?"

"*Soy yo, señor*. Macías. The wagon driver, me."

Jay remembered the kind Mexican who had given him and Tuck a ride against mine regulations — against Lamon regulations.

"What are you doing here?"

A ghostly face drew close to the bars, a pale patch in the gloom. "I no — I not speak good *inglés* but I got — I want tell you —"

"Wait a minute." Jay heard a squeak as a chair was pushed back in the jail office; the yellow glow of a lantern suffused the mud bricks of the hallway. "Someone's coming!"

"What's going on in here?" A key clicked in the lock. Silhouetted against the light, a burly figure stood in the doorway, pistol at the ready. It was not the old man who had brought them supper. "Who the hell were you talking to?"

"No one," Jay lied. "I was just looking out the window at the night — the stars." He heard a quick shuffling noise and knew that Macías had fled.

The visitor, a stocky man with a pepper-and-salt beard, ran to the window. Peering into the night, he squeezed off a shot. "God damn — I think I seen him! Skittering off like a scalded cat!" Holding the lantern in the other hand, he stared at Jay accusingly. "Who the hell was it?"

Awakened by the shot, Tuck sat up, clutching the blanket about his belly. "Don't shoot!"

"I don't know who it was," Jay faltered. "I mean — I think I heard a voice, but I'm not sure. Maybe there was someone there. But I sure don't know anyone around here."

The jailer was still suspicious. Heavy-footed, he prowled about the cell, throwing blankets aside, casting the rays of the lamp into dark corners. A scorpion paused in the yellow glow, lifted its tail menacingly, then disappeared into a chink in the mud bricks.

"All right," the man grumbled. "Guess no harm was did. You fellers can go back to sleep." Locking the cell door, he clumped heavily away.

"What the hell was that all about?" Tuck asked.

"Nothing."

Yawning, Tuck knuckled his short-cropped white hair. "Lordy, Lordy, did I ever have a bad dream!"

"So did I." Jay did not think it useful to tell Tuck about Macías. Nothing had come of it anyway.

The rest of the night passed without incident. Jay slept, or thought he did. Aware at last of a lightening of the gloom, he got up to relieve himself in the bucket. After a gap-toothed yawn and a few grunts, Tuck woke also. He rose, scratching himself. "That pie sets kind of heavy on my stomach." Still scratching, he shambled to the window. For a long moment he stood, peering out. Slowly the monkeylike scratching ceased. "Jesus H. Christ and all the Apostles!"

In the faint flush of a July dawn, sky soft with banners of pink and purple and rose, the open space between the jail and the river had a ghostlike appearance, remindful of woodcuts of old Pompeii. There were newly carpentered booths, gay with bunting; a rude arena with a tall post set in the ground, probably greased; a flag drooped from the top of the pole. But what made Jay suck in his breath was the structure occupying the center of the burned plain.

"Now look at that, will you!" Tuck's voice was incredulous. "There ain't any length those bastards won't go to to plague us!"

The platform of old mine timbers was about six feet off the burned grasses, with a rude stairs leading up. Two stout vertical beams thrust up from the platform, and across them was another. From the horizontal beam dangled two nooses.

Jay's voice rose in panic. "Tuck, they're really going to do it! They're going to hang us!"

"No they ain't!" Tuck's voice was uncertain.

"They wouldn't go to all that trouble if they —"

Tuck slapped him hard across the face. "Stop that caterwauling! It's just part of the fun, don't you see? There ain't no jurisdiction can hang a man for what we done!"

Jay backed away from the window and sat on the cot. "But the fact is — you don't know any more about it than I do! This is an evil place, a kind of throwback! I felt it the minute we rode in here! There's some kind of evil spell, I tell you! You just don't understand like I do!"

Tuck's voice was harsh. "And I ain't scroobling around like no chicken with its head cut off, neither!"

Jay wet dry lips. "Maybe it doesn't worry you all that much. You're an old man, sixty or more, and —"

"Fifty-seven!"

"Most of your life has run out but I'm young!" A tremor came into Jay's voice. "I'm only twenty-five! I can't feel as careless as you about a thing like this!"

"A year is gold to me like it is to you!" Tuck picked up a piece of gristly and grease-iced meat from the night before. "Now just you don't worry, pardner! There's rough times ahead, but we'll win out!"

Full day finally came, bathing the festive grounds in bright sunshine. People began to straggle onto the scene, some on foot, some mounted, with a sprinkling of buggies, traps, and wagons. A man sat on the steps of the gibbet and blew tentatively on a fife. Another in a red shako joined him, carrying a cornet. At a long table aproned workers hacked chunks of beef and lamb from bloody carcasses and spitted them over a bed of coals, uncovered with a shovel.

"Barbecue!" Tuck sniffed, licked his lips. "Smell that sauce they're basting it with!"

Jay wasn't hungry. The pulse thudded heavily in his ear. He counted: *one, two, three* — The rhythmic pulse missed a beat, then another. *One, two, three* — "I'm going to faint," he said.

"No you ain't. You never eat more 'n a bite last night. You're just hungry."

Maybe his heart *would* stop, releasing him quickly and mercifully from this bad dream. Dully he sensed voices from the deputy's office. Otherwise they seemed abandoned, already entombed.

Tuck went to the window. "There must be a couple hundred people out there, milling around like ants at a picnic!"

Time dragged on. The sun reached the zenith. Bars of sunlight finally crosshatched the cell floor. The band started to play a military march. Jay knew music, but didn't recognize the tune. Then the band swung joyfully into "Camptown Races":

> "*Camptown ladies sing this song,*
> *Doo dah, doo dah,*
> *Camptown Racetrack five miles long,*
> *Oh, doo dah day!*"

At booted steps in the corridor he started nervously. The deputy stood there, grave and solemn, with the grizzled jailer of the night before. The old man called Polonius handed the deputy a ring of keys. "I don't think this is right, Mr. Wagstaff! My advice'd be to —"

"You're not paid for advice," the deputy said coldly. "You're mostly paid to sweep out the jail, old man."

Mumbling, Polonius stood aside. The deputy stepped into the cell. "You folks ready to go? It's almost three."

Tuck was defiant. "No, we *ain't* ready to go! By God, I'm a citizen in good standing of Coffee County, Tennessee, and my congressman is a-goin' to hear about this shivaree!"

The deputy and his stocky assistant, carrying a shotgun, led them out into the ankle-deep dust of River Street. With the barrel of the shotgun they were nudged around the corner of the jail and down the sloping sunbaked plain toward the river. Wide-eyed and silent, a gaggle of small boys followed. As they passed through the crowd, talking and joking ceased. Many of the spectators were white, in dress-up clothes, but most were Mexican *mineros* — miners — and millworkers, along with a few inscrutable Indians. As the little group passed the dark men took off straw hats; women in flowing colorful skirts and dark rebozo shawls crossed themselves and hugged fat babies tighter. Their faces were somber.

"Up there," the deputy instructed, pointing.

The band stopped playing, trailing off in a discordant note. Jay hesitated at the bottom of the rude steps, shading his eyes against the sun. Was this truly happening? The stocky man gave him a shove. "Up! Up!" The deputy took Jay's arm, adding, "We haven't got all day, you know. There's the barbecue and the fireworks."

On the platform Tuck stared contemptuously at the crowd. "Ain't you got any decency?" he shouted. "It ain't right to do this to a human!"

The crowd stared back with glazed intensity. No one spoke, jeered, said anything; there was only the upturned sea of faces. In a daze Jay stared back. At the fringe of the crowd was a well-cared-for Whitechapel surrey, standing aside from the general press of traps, buggies, and Democrat wagons. The surrey was painted a light blue, with light-blue dusters, and the moldings were emphasized by a single cream stripe. Lounging on the gaily striped cushions was a lady in a flowered Leghorn hat, bright parasol like a scepter in her hand. She seemed incredibly far away, an image through the small end of a telescope. Like such an image, however, her features were preternaturally clear and sharp to Jay's stunned gaze. The face was as fine chiseled as an expensive cut-glass candy dish; blond hair fell luxuriously over her shoulders. He watched her with glazed eyes, willing himself to see nothing else, to feel nothing else, to know nothing else. Was it not reasonable to think that such a teeming brain, filled with that talismanic image, could not possibly be snuffed into nothingness by a hempen loop? Already they were pinioning Tuck's hands behind his back.

"Lady —" Jay murmured. It was a prayer. Through the small end of the telescope he thought she was smiling at him. Reassurance, or —

"Now you," the deputy said casually.

When the stocky man reached for his wrists, truth suddenly burned through Jay's catalepsy. With a surge

33

of strength he knocked the deputy aside, started to vault over the edge of the platform. But the stocky man caught his shirttail and dragged him back, holding him while the unruffled deputy bound his wrists. The noose dropped over his head, and he felt the bite of the coarse rope on his neck.

"Right under the ear," the deputy mused, giving the eight-banded loop a final adjustment. "Now you just let yourself go limp, boy — don't fight it. Before you know, it will all be over."

Jay begged for his life. "Don't, please — don't! I don't want to die! I didn't do anything — it was Tuck that stole the silver! I'll do anything —"

"Shut up!" Tuck snarled. "God damn it, stop your sniveling! Don't give them the satisfaction!"

Jay was still screaming when the implacable deputy sprang the trap at a few minutes past three in the afternoon. The door dropped; there was a strange sound from the crowd. As the rope tightened Jay had one last crystalline view of the lady in the Whitechapel surrey; the lady watching, wheat-yellow hair spilling out from under the Leghorn hat, parasol aloft. Was she smiling still?

The rest was nothingness.

CHAPTER
THREE

In the foothills around the mine shafts lay patches of snow that did not melt in the thin winter sunshine. A heavy blanket mantled the distant peaks. At night, even with the moderating influence of the river, the thermometer dropped to near the freezing point. Below ground, in the shafts and tunnels of the Lamon mines, the temperature rose sharply; the Mexican miners labored night and day in 100-degree heat. No white man, it was said, could long work in that dust-laden stifling atmosphere. Too, there were frequent breakthroughs into pockets of hot water that scalded men. Rotten timbers collapsed, crushing the miners, and in the reducing mill frequent accidents injured still more. Ordinarily the *mineros* were meek and peaceable, but of late they had been showing signs of disquiet, Mr. Dineen reported. Accordingly, Andrew Lamon had been persuaded to hire a doctor for Mohave City.

Dr. Carmody was a slender bearded man with a scholarly look. He had seen Mr. Andrew Lamon's advertisement in the San Francisco *Call* offering a stipend of fifty dollars per month from the Lamon Mining and Milling Corporation to attend to their employees' injuries and illnesses, plus free office space, living quarters, and all the fees from his treatment of private citizens. "Mohave City," the advertisement went on, "is favorably situated on the banks of the Colorado River. The air is dry and healthful and the surroundings pleasing to the eye. The citizens are prosperous, thanks to the Lamon Mining and Milling Corporation, which is the principal employer. Veins currently being worked assay over sixty ounces of gold to the ton, promising rapid growth and progress for the region."

Carmody turned a quizzical eye on his surroundings. "Primitive, isn't it? The office and living quarters, I mean."

"I know it doesn't look like much," Mr. Dineen admitted, "but I'll have old Polonius come in and clean it up. You'll need a sign, too. How do you want it to read?"

Carmody peered through a grimy window, rubbed at the dirt with a gloved hand. "'J. B. Carmody — Physician and Surgeon.' That will do nicely." He dusted his hands. "My valise and the boxes with my instruments and medical supplies are still at the landing where the *Cocopah* dropped them off. Could someone see they are picked up and brought here?"

Dineen was a large and handsome man with a flowing red beard. Superintendent of the mines and the mill, he wore a white suit and sateen cravat better suited to a desert summer than to the present chill.

"I'll take care of it," he promised, making an entry in a notebook. "Now let's see . . ." He pondered. "The mines own a big deposit of coal back in the hills. That's how we power the hoisting machines and the stamp mill. So we'll see you have coal for your stove. There's a cot in the back room where you can sleep if you want, and out behind is a privy. If you're not inclined to rough it, Mrs. Yount up the street boards white people. She sets a good table: pie and fried chicken every Sunday. There's the Chinaman's, too, but I don't favor his cooking. Cheap, though."

Dr. Carmody nodded, pleasantly. "I guess I was lucky I saw Mr. Lamon's advertisement." There was no sarcasm in his voice. At least, Emmett Dineen could detect none.

After the superintendent left, Dr. Carmody sat in a rump-sprung chair, rocking. A small and torpid lizard huddled on the removable lid atop the stove. Another curled about a rusty coffeepot. Spider webs hung like lace curtains over the dirty windows, and the air smelled dead and dusty. The boards of the floor were worn and split; in one place withered summer grasses poked through. "This is it," he murmured, looking about. "This is Mohave City; this is the place."

From his half reverie he was awakened by pounding on the boardwalk outside. He opened the door to find a lean gray-muzzled man nailing up a makeshift sign. Satisfied, the ancient stuck his claw hammer into a leather apron and climbed down the ladder. "That suit you, Doc?"

Stepping into the scanty sunlight, Dr. Carmody gazed upward. J. B. CARMODY — PHYSICION AND SIRGEON. At least the name was spelled right. "I guess so," he said. "For the time being, anyway. Thank you, Mr. —"

"Polonius. That's what they call me." Taking off his faded blue Union cap, the old man followed him into the office. "Is your hours right now?"

"I haven't established my office hours yet. What ails you?"

"It ain't me — it's my woman, Mabel. She runs the boardinghouse up the street."

Dr. Carmody remembered. "That would be Mrs. Yount, then. And you're Polonius — Yount."

"Yes, sir. I help out around here. Anything you want, just yell for Polonius. But Mabel, y' see — sometimes, after cooking and making beds and all, she gets plumb wore out. Says her heart is acting up."

"Well," Dr. Carmody said, "bring her in later and I'll examine her. But — where did you get that name — I mean 'Polonius'?"

The old man kicked sheepishly at the withered summer grasses. "It's a name Mr. Dineen hung on me once, and I guess it kind of took. I'm always giving people advice, he says. Seems there was a character in some old play that was named Polonius, and he always —"

"I know," the doctor said.

Waiting for his things to arrive, Dr. Carmody took up his gold-headed walking stick to stroll about the town and introduce himself to the citizens. A tall and slender figure in black frock coat and bowler hat, he nodded pleasantly to his future patients. In Hagop Aroutunian's Climax Store he bought a cigar. In the window of the Star Livery Stable a man writing in a ledger looked up and waved; most Mohave City people had already heard about him, he supposed. At the Empire Saloon a pig-faced man stacking beer barrels called to him.

"You the new doc, mister?"

"I am."

In spite of the chill wind from the river, the burly man was sweating. Wiping palms on a dirty shirt, he extended his hand. "Monk Griffin, Doc! If you're a drinking man, it's always on the house at the Empire, whatever you want."

At the landing below, the *Cocopah* swung in the gangplank and blew her whistle, ready to steam upriver; all the way to Hardyville, in Mormon territory, Captain Thorne had told him.

Swinging his gold-headed stick, Dr. Carmody came at last to the end of the graded road. Beyond, it dwindled to a narrow lane winding down a canyon toward the river. Passing a gaggle of curious goats, he found himself among the tin-roofed mud huts and sagging lean-tos of Mex Town, where the miners lived; Mex Town, poor and squalid, smelling of stale urine and unwashed bodies. Somewhere a guitar twanged off key and woodsmoke curled into the air, a merciful veil over the huddled dwellings.

When he returned, boxes and cartons were stacked in the front room of his new habitation. Rolling up his sleeves, he started to work. Borrowing a hammer and nails from the proprietor of the American Eagle Barbershop next door, he opened the crates, using the scrap lumber to fashion crude shelves. Finding a scraggly broom in a corner, he sprinkled water on the floor and swept out. Putting two boxes together, he made a rude examining table in the back room. Another large box would serve as a desk. He pried a kerosene lamp on a swinging bracket from a wall and reinstalled it over the examining table, reminding himself to buy kerosene from the Climax Store. He was arranging medical books on one of the shelves when the door opened.

A young lady stood in the doorway. She was modishly attired in a green paletot; the muslin waist was a bright print, with sprigs of holly. The large felt hat was ornamented with straw flowers, and tipped at an angle to display a chignon of blond hair caught up in a net.

"Ma'am?" Dr. Carmody said politely. He appreciated what he saw; he had an eye for good fashion.

"I'm Flora Lamon."

He indicated the sagging chair. "Won't you please come in?"

Swinging a beaded reticule, she strolled about the room, head cocked at an angle, gray eyes taking everything in. "It's not much, is it, Doctor?"

He agreed. "But I intend to improve it as I have time."

When she sat down, one dainty booted foot crossed over the other, he added, "I'm Dr. Carmody, ma'am. J. B. Carmody."

"I know."

"I — I —" When she smiled, it disconcerted him. "Mr. Andrew Lamon hired me."

"I know that too. Father told me."

"Well, ma'am, I'm glad to be here. I — I've been out of practice for some time — an incapacitating illness. But now I am recovered, and consider myself fortunate to have been chosen by Mr. Lamon."

She pursed her lips wryly. "I don't know whether you're fortunate or not, sir! At any rate, you were the only one to apply! Mohave City is not Park Avenue in New York, you must know. Father won't like me to have said that, though. Mohave City is his creation, and he is very proud of it." Taking off the hat, she laid it carefully in her lap, shaking her head as if grateful for relief from its constriction. "What does the J. B. stand for, pray?"

He was bemused, watching the wheat-gold mass of hair stirring about the nape of her neck. "Eh?"

"The initials! Your initials, Doctor! What do they stand for?"

"Ah — James Carmody, ma'am. James Baker Carmody." To cover his discomfiture he half sat on the edge of his desk-crate, propped on hands behind his back. "Is that where you live, then — the big house on the hill?"

"Yes. Father and I, that is." She sighed, and removed her long gloves. "Just the two of us. You see, I was educated in the East, and only recently returned — home. Back there, there were balls and parties and things, but there's little of that here. Most of the white people are busy at the mines or the mill. When the sun goes down they're too tired to do anything. But I'm glad we have at least one new face in town!" Carefully she put on her hat, folded the gloves, and put them in her reticule. "Oh — I almost forgot! You're to come to supper tonight! Father wants to meet you."

He felt a small tremor in his chest. "I had hoped to get things arranged and make myself presentable before I had the privilege of meeting your father, ma'am." He waved at his rough carpentry. "There's so much to do, and since I haven't yet had time to unpack my personal things, you see me still in traveling garments, which are dusty and rather wrinkled. Perhaps later —"

"Nonsense! Supper is at eight! There will be other guests also, citizens of the town. Amalia — our cook — has laid on a fine meal: Guaymas shrimp, *poulet à l'orange*, a roast of beef, berry tarts, and the proper wines. We'll expect you by seven-thirty, at least, for a little conversation before supper."

He bowed. "A pleasure, ma'am."

At the door she paused, thoughtful. "I don't want to presume, Doctor, on such short acquaintance, but perhaps I can offer friendly advice."

"Of course, ma'am."

"My father built the Mohave City mines into a corporation traded upon at the New York Stock Exchange. Last year the firm shipped out over fifty thousand ounces of pure gold. You will find him an unusual man. And the best way to get along with Andrew Lamon is to do what he asks."

He was surprised at the abrupt words, and started to speak. But Flora Lamon had gone, with a gay smile. Quickly she walked up the boardwalk, humming a little tune and swinging the beaded bag by its golden chain.

⋆ ⋆ ⋆

For the invitation to supper Dr. Carmody put on his linen shirt with the starched cuffs. Painstakingly he blacked his boots and rubbed Ruby Dress Pomade into his short-cropped hair, which often refused to lie flat. Polonius brought a basin of hot water from the Chinaman's and sat in the office delivering homilies while Dr. Carmody bathed in a tin tub.

"Cleanliness is next to godliness, Mabel says. Guess I'm a long ways from heaven, then. On the other hand, I might say it's plumb unnatural to wash so much. Animals don't wash much, and they're the Lord's creatures too — except cats, they wash theirselves a lot. But you take —"

"Bring me my pants, please, Polonius," Dr. Carmody asked. "They're hanging over the back of the chair."

The old man stood back and admired the final ensemble. "Doc, you're surely a handsome man! Didn't no female ever set her cap for you?"

"A few. Now hand me my bowler, will you?"

"Your what?"

"My hat, there on the shelf. And the walking stick, if you please."

"Walking stick? Ain't you going to ride up there?"

"Ride?"

"Mine company got a horse and trap for you at Hodge's Livery. Didn't no one tell you?"

"No. Well, walking is good exercise. Good for the heart, the liver, the general health."

Adjusting the angle of the bowler in the cracked mirror over the washstand Polonius had found for him, he was finally satisfied.

"I don't know about walking," Polonius muttered as he was leaving. "Animals walks, men rides. That's what makes us human beings, ain't it?"

Dr. Carmody turned down the wick of the kerosene lamp to a thin blue line. "There are other things in heaven and earth, Polonius. Good night, and thank you for your help."

Winter darkness had come; the night was chill. Gratefully he drew the thin sharp air into his lungs, looking upward at pinpricks of steely light peppering the night. A crescent of moon hung low in the west, a single bright star — a planet, he supposed — near its cusp. A conjunction, astronomers called that, the drawing near of the star to the moon. And now there was coming another conjunction. Dr. J. B. Carmody was approaching his destiny.

The pillared mansion blazed with lights. Buggies with patient sleepy-eyed horses were tied to the hitching post. A single well-formed buckskin rolled its eyes and shied when he approached. "Whoa, old girl," he said, and rubbed the velvet muzzle. He had always been good with horses; cows, too, and farm animals in general.

The door was open. Taking off his hat, he stepped inside. The carpet of the anteroom was deep-textured Oriental pile that glowed in rich colors under the hanging lamp with its polished crystal pendants. From the parlor he could hear the sound of a violin, well played, and the murmur of conversation.

"Dr. Carmody!" Awkwardly holding his hat and stick, he turned. "We've been waiting! Everyone is so anxious to meet you!"

"Miss Lamon." He bent to kiss her hand. "I didn't mean to delay the festivities. I walked, you see, but it was farther than I thought, and uphill. It took longer than I intended."

Taking his hand, she led him into the parlor. He was aware of the softness of her hand and the perfume that rose from her bosom. The long China silk dress was belted high under her breast with a chain, the wheaten hair caught back with an Egyptian-looking clasp, showing the high brow and chiseled features to advantage. "Father," she said, "this is Dr. Carmody. He and I have already met, you know."

Andrew Lamon was a craggy man with bushy black eyebrows and a saturnine face. Dr. Carmody judged him to be in his early fifties or thereabouts; a kind of raw energy seemed to emanate from him. The hand clasped around the champagne glass was big and knobby. When he offered the other to Dr. Carmody it hinted of great strength.

"So this is the sawbones I hired! Welcome to Mohave City, sir — welcome to the Lamon Mining and Milling Corporation, and to my home!"

Dr. Carmody bowed. He had practiced it often, and managed quite well.

"This is my superintendent, Emmett Dineen; you two have already met. Deputy Wagstaff, all the way from Prescott to keep order in our little community. Mr. and Mrs. Hodge — Luke handles our animals, and runs the livery and feed store. Major Iredale — Sarah over there is his daughter. She plays the violin well. Teaches school, too!"

Dineen was in a fresh white suit with a flower in the buttonhole. Wagstaff was a slender man in a well-cut nankeen suit, with dark unrevealing eyes. Hodge was a colorless man of middle age, with a stout red-faced wife who beamed at the doctor and assured him she would surely visit him soon for her catarrh. Major Iredale was an elderly Civil War veteran who seemed slightly confused. His daughter Sarah — a plain girl in a drab dress, hair drawn tightly back in a knot — held bow and violin in one hand while she guided the major's hesitant arm with the other. "Shake hands, Papa. This is Dr. Carmody, the new doctor in town."

For all his apparent woolgathering, the old man's faded eyes were sharp and observant. He stared at Dr. Carmody for a long time, holding the doctor's hand in a surprisingly strong grip. When Sarah said softly, "Papa —" her father dropped the grip, saying, "You remind me of someone, sir."

"Yes?" Dr. Carmody's tone was casual.

"Regimental surgeon of the Sixteenth Mississippi. Built like you, sir — tall, not much heft to him, pointed little beard, real good hands, whether they were on a horse or a wounded man. He —"

"Shall we go into supper?" Flora Lamon interrupted. She took Dr. Carmody's arm, and Andrew Lamon on her other. Mr. and Mrs. Hodge followed, then Sarah

46

and the major, with Emmett Dineen and Deputy Wagstaff bringing up the rear. They were murmuring to each other, and Dr. Carmody wondered if they were discussing him; he thought they were.

The shrimp were large and sweet and cold, brought up in iced barrels on the *Cocopah*. The chicken was tender and succulent in an unusual orange sauce, and the beef crusty on the outside, faintly pink within. The wines were French; Chablis chilled with snow from the mountains, he was told, the Burgundy rich and full-bodied.

"Delicious!" Dr. Carmody announced, touching his lips with a crested napkin of finest linen. "For a plain country doctor, this *is* a treat!"

Flora Lamon leaned forward in the candlelight. The yellow light bathed her shoulders and breast in a lambent glow. *Beautiful*, Dr. Carmody thought, *but somehow flawed*. Flawed? In what way? He was not sure, did not even know why he had thought such a thing. Still —

"Dr. Carmody!"

He started. "Ma'am, excuse me! I — I — well, I suppose I was so overcome by the cuisine that I was still savoring it! You spoke to me?"

She laughed. "You were in a brown study! I was just saying that I — Father and I — hope you will come to visit us often."

"I shall be pleased, ma'am."

After supper Andrew Lamon took foil-wrapped cigars from a tray the Mexican maid handed him. "Now, ladies, perhaps you will join each other in the parlor while the menfolk have their brandy and cigars. Dr. Carmody, will you join me in the library upstairs? I would like to talk to you about the company and your new obligations."

The gentlemen rose. The ladies drifted off, chatting. Wagstaff, Dineen, Hodge, and Major Iredale lit cigars and sat down again, watching while a servingman in a white coat poured brandy into polished snifters.

Upstairs, Dr. Carmody and Andrew Lamon sat in the paneled library sipping their brandy poured from a cut-glass bottle with a gold stopper in the form of a lion's head. Through the window Dr. Carmody saw a shred of moon caught in the lace curtains; from below sounded the incessant clatter of the mill.

"I must tell you, Dr. Carmody," Andrew Lamon said, "that hiring a physician for the mines did not seem to me to be a good idea. The Mexicans are tough, healthy people. Oh, at times there is an accident, I grant you! But tragic as it is to tell, the people are generally killed, or crushed beyond repair, so a physician is a needless extravagance. But my daughter Flora talked me into it. Some of the miners — troublemakers down in Mex Town — have been agitating for a doctor as well as a priest. Flora took their side." He chewed on the cigar; the coal brightened under the shadow of the Argand lamp. "She is a stubborn girl, that daughter of mine! Flora's mother and I are — separated. I have had my hands full with Flora. Nevertheless —" He broke off, musingly watching the gray curl of smoke from the prime Havana tobacco. "So now we have a mine physician,

48

and surgeon." Eyes half hidden under the shaggy brows, he peered at Dr. Carmody. "I read your letters, of course, but I do not want there to be any misunderstandings. So please state again your qualifications."

Dr. Carmody cleared his throat. "I will, of course, hang my framed diploma on the wall of my office, as is customary. As I said in my letter, I graduated from the San Francisco College of Homeopathic Medicine and Surgery six years ago with a speciality in surgery of the bones and ligaments. I practiced in that city for two years, and then was diagnosed as suffering from the consumption. I came to the Arizona Territory for my health, and am now completely cured. In the interim I worked at various odd jobs to support myself, including that of a pharmacist. However, I am now fit again, and anxious to resume my legitimate practice."

Up the stairway, through the closed door, came the reedlike melody of the violin and the sound of laughter. The ladies and gentlemen were probably dancing a mazurka. Andrew Lamon drummed bony fingers on the desk; Dr. Carmody noticed a vein throbbing in his temple. "Anything more you care to tell me, sir?"

"What more would you like to know?"

"Family? Ever married? Drink laudanum, like some of the doctor johnnies do?"

Stiffly the doctor said, "I have no family except a few scattered cousins in Ohio whom I hardly know. I have had — relations with a few women, but do not consider myself a womanizer. I do not drink laudanum, nor do I approve of those who do. Mr. Lamon, your questions seem to hint at some mystery! I assure you there is none, and if my answers do not satisfy you —"

"There, there, now!" Lamon rose, stubbing out the half-smoked cigar. "You satisfy me, Doctor, you surely do! In time you will come to understand that my manner is meant only to be businesslike!" He held out a big-knuckled hand, the back streaked with dark hairs. "Dance, do you?" He opened the door; the lively violin and the stamp of boots drifted up the grand stairway. "I vow Flora is getting anxious for you to join her do-si-do or whatever it is called!"

They were halfway down the stairs when the violin and the dancing stopped, the music trailing off in a sudden rasp. On the landing, among the giant potted ferns and the oil portraits of what were probably Lamon ancestors, Andrew Lamon paused, listening. "The mill's stopped!"

Below them Emmett Dineen stood in the open doorway. Beside him cowered a Mexican boy in ragged *manta* pants, holding a tattered straw hat to his chest as if deriving protection from it.

"Luis here says a man's caught in the belt to the shaker tables at the mill!" Dineen called up to them. "I'll go down and see what I can do!"

Andrew Lamon went carefully down the grand staircase. "Damned rascals! We're committed to five thousand ounces this month, and some jackass has to go and get tangled up in the belts! Well —" He turned to Dr. Carmody. "It appears this is the first chance to show your skills, Doctor. But watch out for

50

malingering! Mexicans are naturally lazy, and will do anything to avoid a job of work!"

"I'll do my best," Dr. Carmody promised, "but first I'll have to stop at my office and pick up my bag."

"I'll drive you down in my buckboard," Dineen offered.

He was aware of the rest of the guests in the hallway, clustered about and murmuring. "My goodness!" the plump Mrs. Hodge clucked. "Seems someone's *always* getting hurt in that mill, or in one of the mines!" When her husband frowned at her, she subsided. Major Iredale did not seem to understand what was going on, and his daughter tried to explain. The deputy stood silently to one side, chewing on his cigar.

"You'd better come along too, Wagstaff," Dineen said abruptly, eyeing him and Flora. "They're restless, you know, and there may be trouble."

A glance passed between the deputy and Flora Lamon. "Yes," she agreed. "The doctor may need help."

Dr. Carmody thanked his hostess. "I'm sorry this had to come up, ma'am."

She smiled. "Another time, then? Soon!"

They went into the dark night. Dineen untied the reins and climbed into the seat; Dr. Carmody followed. The mine superintendent drove slowly, horses only shambling down the road toward the town and the lighted mill.

"Hadn't we better hurry?" Dr. Carmody asked.

Dineen shrugged, touched the flank of the near horse with his whip.

"Who's that?" Dr. Carmody looked over his shoulder at the silent figure trotting after them on the skittish buckskin.

Dineen didn't turn. "Wagstaff," he said, and seemed amused.

"Oh!" Dr. Carmody had forgotten the taciturn deputy.

They stopped to pick up his black bag, and finally reached the mill. Men stood outside, holding lanterns to fight their way. "*Dese prisa!*" someone cried. *Hurry!* Then, when Emmett Dineen's red beard showed in the rays of the lanterns — "*Por favor, señor!*" *Please.*

Climbing down from the buckboard, Dr. Carmody smelled again the rank juices of the mill — caustic chemicals, coal smoke, steam, sweat. *This is the first chance to show your skills to us, Doctor.* It was; he had better show a proper medical training.

CHAPTER
FOUR

In the night the Lamon mill took on the appearance of Hades. There was a stench of chemical tanks, flaring torches, people running about, hissing of steam, excited and staccato Spanish. A pall of smoke and cinders settled down from the great engine that powered the mill. Now it idled, slide valves and push rods creeping almost imperceptibly in oiled slots.

"Get out of the way!" Dineen snapped, walking before Jay like the prow of a ship breasting the sea. "God damn it, stop that jabbering! A man can hardly think!" Over his shoulder he gestured at Jay. "Here, along the catwalk!"

Overhead hung the festooning of leather belts which carried power from the steam engine to the conveyors, shaker tables, and other devices that wrested gold from the parent ore. From a high pulley, smoothed by long slapping of the belt, a mahogany-dark leather band dropped down to operate the Wilfley tables, the shakers that separated crushed ore by intrinsic weight; it hung motionless, clutch of the big engine disengaged. In a slurry of sand and gravel lay a young man, eyes closed, face grimacing in pain.

"Stand clear!" Dineen ordered. "Here's the doctor!"

As the workers pressed back, Jay saw that the boy's leg had been crushed between the vertical belt and the big pulley that powered the shaker table. Body wedged in the beams supporting the table, the young man had been caught while the belt ground on.

"You, Macías!" Dineen said sharply. He pushed aside the burly man who knelt at the youth's side, lantern in hand. "Give the doctor room, do you hear me?"

The man called Macías got up slowly and deliberately. "*Es mi sobrino*," he said. "Paco, my nephew."

"I don't care if it's your mother!" Dineen barked. "Get the hell out of the way — all of you!"

Macías, Jay thought. It was a common name in the Territory; there were a lot of Macíases. Gingerly he bent over the boy and opened the black satchel. "Here," he said, taking out a bottle. "Paco, drink a little of this and you'll feel better." To Dineen he explained, "Tincture of laudanum, for the pain." In spite of queasiness he forced himself to examine the torn leg. A wave of nausea washed his stomach, and he felt faint. To cover his discomfiture he spoke to the boy's uncle. "Shine your lantern over this way so I can have a better look."

In the flickering rays he inspected the damage. The leg had been cruelly mauled by the friction of the belt. The flesh was torn away, the small bone — the fibula, was that it? — yes, the fibula, the other one was the tibia — the fibula had been shattered and the splinters poked bloodily out. God, what a thing to confront an amateur surgeon this first day in Mohave City!

"He's bleeding badly," he muttered. "I can't get at anything till someone starts the engine so I can pull the leg out from between the belt and the pulley." Getting an arm under the body, he nodded to Macias, who took up the rest of the weight in hairy muscular arms. "Tell the engineer to back off."

Dineen spoke to a white man in a ragged silk shirt, gaudy stripes an odd contrast to the oil-stained fabric. "Ike, crack the steam a bit in reverse — slow, like the doctor says!"

The idling engine hissed. The man called Ike pulled a lever, and the great tangle of overhead belts began to move. The pulley of the shaker table turned. Paco's body shuddered in their grasp. *Madre de Dios! Ay, que dolor!*"

"It's coming!" Jay muttered. "Careful! Take the weight off the other limb! There! Lay him down — easy now!"

For the first time he noticed the deputy in the lanternlit circle of faces. Wagstaff watched the scene with curious intentness; absorbed, yet somehow detached. Dineen spoke to the deputy but Wagstaff did not seem to hear.

Quickly Jay slit the torn pants leg with his penknife and knotted his handkerchief around the thigh, tying a hard knot to press tightly against the big blood-vessel. He was glad he remembered that trick, and glad also he knew where the damned artery was. In his mind's eye he saw page 367 of Heaton's *Compendium of Surgical Practice*, the book that had cost him three dollars, used, at the medical bookstore near the Bella Union

Music Hall at Washington and Kearny Streets. He had been more penniless than a real medical student, but somehow he scraped up the money. Page 367 — *V. Femoralis, V. Cava Inferior, V. Renalis* — he had memorized them all.

"Do you have a litter of some sort?"

Shrugging, Dineen spoke to a mill hand. "Get a board someplace, a wide board."

Macías tugged at Jay's sleeve. "Take him my house, *señor doctor?*"

Jay remembered Mex Town, squalid and dirty — slinking dogs, urine-smelling rivulets in the street, hovering flies.

"No," he said, rolling down blood-spattered sleeves. "There's this room behind my office. We'll take him there."

"He — Paco live?"

Jay watched the man return with two narrow planks, hastily nailed together with crosswise battens. "I can't promise anything," he said, shaking his head. "If you're a good Catholic, I'd advise praying!"

The clear blue dusk of early evening had given way to a murky sky. A crescent moon showed chill and wan. As they carried Paco down the steps into the street, a misty rain began to fall. Macías and another mill hand handled the litter carefully, speaking in soft Spanish to the boy, his mangled limb bound with Jay's walking stick for splint. Dineen, Deputy Wagstaff beside him on the broad porch before the mill, looked down at them almost casually.

"Are you coming?" Jay asked.

Dineen made a sucking sound with his teeth. "What for?"

"Aren't you interested in how this turns out? I mean — don't you have to make some sort of report to Mr. Lamon?"

"Let me know in the morning," Dineen said. "Time enough!"

As the procession moved away Jay was aware Dineen and the deputy were talking together. He heard only one word — "feisty," it sounded like.

"Careful," he said to Macías. Remembering some Spanish, he repeated, "*Cuidado! Adelante hay un bache en la calle!" There is a hole in the street.*

Feisty! He had never been called that before. Always he had been a quiet, civil person, patient under provocation. In spite of the coming test under the bracketed green kerosene lamp in his office, he almost smiled. During the months in San Francisco he had changed a lot. They, too, would change, all of them, he would see to that. As yet he had no firm plan; each case would probably require a different treatment. He would punish them: Dineen, the deputy, the kangaroo court that had condemned him — all!

In Columbus Jay had been apprenticed to an ancient druggist who doubled in abortions and jackleg surgery. Old Doc Clevenger (the title was honorary) did embalming also at reasonable rates. Jay, studying for his own pharmacist's license, assisted Doc, sometimes being himself trusted with the knife. But he had never before cut into a warm and living human being.

57

Months before, hired to sweep out and do odd jobs around the San Francisco College of Homeopathic Medicine and Surgery, he had often sneaked unseen into the back of the surgical amphitheater to watch the professors dissect cadavers for the instruction of the medical students leaning over the high-banked railings. No one noticed the shabbily clad young man as intent as they on the sweeping incisions, the careful lifting aside and out of organs, separation and identification of threadlike nerves. Once, on a dark and rainy night, foghorns booming in the bay, Jay even gained entry into the ice-cooled room where the school kept cadavers. Secondhand scalpel in hand, he had been frightened away by a night watchman. Balked of the opportunity to find out at first hand how the clavicula fit into the humerus, he went back to his painfully acquired medical books. Some he had bought from his meager salary; others good-natured medical students gave him, amused by the shabby young man's interest in medicine. When he had seen Andrew Lamon's advertisement in the San Francisco *Call* he applied immediately. Now, strawlike hair cut short and colored dark brown by applications of Dr. Musgrave's Parisian Tonic, once clean-shaven chin adorned by neatly trimmed mustaches and beard of the same shade, he rolled up his sleeves.

"Get them to stand back, please," he told Macías. "They're crowding me."

"*Me llamo Rubén*," Macías said. "My name is Rubén, *señor*."

"Rubén, then."

58

A throng of Mexicans, men and women, some with hastily awakened children, had tried to follow the litter into the back room of his office; Paco appeared to be a favorite. Now they stood outside in the darkness, patiently waiting. He could not, however, in good conscience refuse admission to Paco's family. There was Paco's mother, a heavy-set black-shawled woman, and her husband, Jorge, along with a limpid-eyed and rosy-skinned young sister with the same glossy ringlets and sensual lips as the injured Paco.

"Sit down here, on these boxes," Jay relented. "And wait — just wait. I'll let you know when there's anything important!"

Paco's father, straw hat in hands, nodded, took his wife's arm and turned away. Jay watched the family sit down with the dumb resignation of poor people in the presence of calamity. Jorge Macías, Paco's father, had given no sign of recognition. Jay remembered the ride into Mohave City on the ore wagon, wondered if Macías had been punished for breaking the rules of the Lamon Mining and Milling Corporation. That night Jorge had covertly come to the jail to tell them something — Jay and Tuck. Had Macías known all along it was all a trumped-up thing, a cruel and inhuman joke?

"Dr. Carmody?"

Paco's breathing slowing under the chloroformed cloth his uncle held over the youth's nose, Jay turned abruptly. "I told you —"

"I — I came. I thought maybe I could help."

Sarah Iredale stood hesitantly in the doorway. "I heard, and thought maybe I — I —"

She was still in the unfashionable dress with the worn lace ruching around the neck. Her hair was awry, twisted into a bun, and she clasped her blue-veined hands anxiously together.

"Back home I helped out in the County Infirmary. I'm not afraid of blood!"

Good Lord, was this going to be a public spectacle? He did not want anyone to witness his incompetence. Rubén Macías, he noticed, kept eyes resolutely averted from the mangled limb. Paco's uncle might faint on him.

"Thank you, Miss Iredale," he said. "Please come in."

"Maybe this will help." Sarah Iredale adjusted the kerosene lamp on its bracket to give better light. Quietly she took the cloth from Rubén Macías, who gratefully retired to the other room.

"Thank you," he said again, and picked up the scalpel.

The job would have daunted a veteran of thirty years in surgical practice. Still and all, Jay knew that much of a surgeon's work was simple mechanics, putting things back into their proper places: measuring, calculating, fitting, like a good tailor fashioning a proper suit of clothes. So long as the patient was kept in that precarious balance between full consciousness and death, so long as the bleeding was stanched, the rest was the work of a carpenter. Pushing the splintered tibia back into place, wrapping it with string in hasty improvisation, he felt a drop of sweat run down his nose. Sarah Iredale caught it with her handkerchief just as it was about to fall into the wound.

He nodded. "We've got to keep the wound clean as we can." One night at the College he had heard the shrieks of a man dying from an infected bowel. It so unnerved him that for three days he would not look at his medical books. But he came back, with steady resolve.

The fibula was more difficult. There was little left, only bits and pieces dotting the mangled flesh. What to do? Nothing in his books had spoken to that question. Finally he decided to take the fibula out altogether. It could do Paco no good, even if he survived.

"Bone saw!" he muttered.

He should have explained more fully, but Sarah Iredale saw the instrument and handed it to him as promptly as would a good surgical nurse. He trimmed the fibula away, and when Paco groaned and the leg quivered he said, "Please — about ten more drops on the cloth from the brown bottle there."

She gave a sudden cry of alarm and set the bottle down. "There — a blood vessel! He's bleeding again!"

Under his breath he cursed. Reaching for the severed tube, he managed to get the slippery thing between his fingers. *Posterior tibial, peroneal, anterior tibial* — he knew the names of all the arteries but had forgotten where this one lay. Knowing the names didn't help; he had somehow to tie it off.

"The thread over there!" he snapped. "The white thread!" Unable to manage with only two hands, he dropped his bone saw. "Can you come in here, Miss Iredale, and take hold of this damned thing while I try to tie it off?"

In the glow of the kerosene lamp her face was pale, but she moved quickly to his side.

"See it? If you can pinch the ends together I can tie it off."

She swallowed — he saw her breast rise and fall quickly under the faded dress — but thrust delicate fingers, the violinist's fingers, into the welter of blood and flesh and fragments of bone. "I've got it, I think."

Their fingers intertwined, he tried to get a loop of thread around the severed artery. Sweat dropped again from his forehead into the wound but there was nothing he could do about it now. Time and again the slippery tube evaded him. He swore fluently, a thing not customary with him. It was not until Jay had been hanged that he took to using some of Tuck Stiles' picturesque oaths.

"I'm sorry, ma'am," he said lamely, "but it's damned difficult! The blasted thing —"

She cleared her throat, spoke apologetically. "Doctor, my fingers are smaller. I do a lot of knitting and sewing and things. Maybe I could —"

"Try it!" he said with some relief. "Here, I'll take the artery!"

In the cramped quarters their bodies touched, drew away, touched again. Her hand was warm against his; in the growing light of dawn he felt cold, and trembled. Gratefully he heard the sound of someone stoking the stove, Polonius Yount's voice as he put chunks of coal into the iron maw.

"I've got it!" Sarah Iredale said. "Do you want to see if I've pulled it tight enough, Doctor?"

He looked. "A good job. A very good job."

Feeling suddenly weary, almost giddy, he put out a hand to steady himself against the sheet-draped wooden boxes. He blinked, trying to seem calm, unruffled.

She glanced at him. "Are you all right?"

"Of course I'm all right! It's just that —"

"Coffee, Doc?" Polonius stood in the doorway, battered tin pot in one hand and a cup in the other. "Brought it from the Chinaman's."

Gratefully Jay took the cup in bloody hands. Then, remembering manners, he offered it to Sarah Iredale. "No," she said quickly. "You need it, Doctor. You're the one that matters."

"I'll get another cup," Polonius offered.

"Are Paco's folks still here?" Jay asked.

"Still here. They ain't gonna leave till it goes one way or t'other."

"Stay with them, will you? Tell them Paco's doing pretty well, considering."

"I'll do 'er," Polonius said. "They're good folks, even if they are greasers."

Jay set down the drained cup. "Now all that's to be done is put in the drains and close." He bent over Paco, lifted an eyelid, stared at the pupil. "Will you give him another few drops, Miss Iredale? I don't want him to wake till it's over."

Revivified by the scalding coffee, he made a final adjustment of bones, ligaments, muscles, and white-sheathed nerves. The torn flesh was like a crazy quilt but at last he stitched it all together, inserted a tubular drain, and neatly bandaged it.

Sarah Iredale supported the limb while he wound linen strips around it. Polonius fashioned rude splints from lumber left over from packing cases, and Jay bound them in place with more linen strips. Paco still slept.

"There!" he said in satisfaction, stepping back to admire his work. Not bad for a nearly pharmacist turned jackleg doctor!

In the gray light of dawn Sarah Iredale's face was worn and haggard. She brushed at the straggling bun of hair. "What will you do with him now? I mean, where will he go?"

"Not to Mex Town!" he said. "At least not for now! I've got to keep an eye on him. The next few days will be critical. Fever, you know, and inflammation."

"There is our house," Sarah Iredale offered. "He can be put in my bed, and I'll sleep on the sofa."

Wiping his hands on a towel, he shook his head. "That's nice of you, ma'am, but I think I'll keep him right here, on the cot." He looked around at the warped boards, gray daylight streaming through chinks, at the dirty muslin ceiling to keep scorpions and spiders from dropping down, at the rain-streaked windows, a pane broken and rags stuffed into the hole. "It isn't much, but I may turn this back room into a hospital. The mill is dangerous, and the mines probably worse." He grinned, feeling light-headed. "How about the Sarah Iredale Memorial Hospital? You did a superb job, ma'am — you've got a way with you!"

She blushed; it was rare he had seen even a touch of color in the pale cheeks.

Paco Macías stirred, groaned.

"He's coming to." Jay called to Polonius and the three lifted Paco and placed him on the sagging cot. "I'll bring you some breakfast, Doc," Polonius promised, and hurried to the Chinaman's.

In the office Paco's relatives still patiently sat, gray lumps in the gray dawn. When Jay came in, sleeves rolled down and his coat on, they stirred. Rubén Macías looked questioningly at him. Jorge Macías stood up, straw hat clutched in workworn hands. They did not speak, only waited with brutelike resignation.

"I've done what I could. I will keep him here for the next few days. There is nothing more to do but wait. Wait, and pray. I cannot promise anything. But Paco is a young man, and healthy. If there are no complications he has a good chance. *Me entienden ustedes?*"

He was unprepared for the sudden action of Paco's mother. Hurrying to him, she knelt to kiss his hand.

"Here, here!" he said in alarm. "*Por favor, señora! No, por favor!*"

Jorge Macías drew her gently up. "*Señor doctor*," he said. "*Gracias.* We all thank you." Groping for words, he put his arm around his wife, while the sister supported her mother on the other side, eyes modestly downcast. "It is good — *bueno* — what you do. *Jamás* — never we have doctor! It — it is good."

65

"You go now," Jay said. "Eat, sleep, pray. *Está en las manos de Dios*. It is in the hands of God."

When he went back into the makeshift surgery Sarah Iredale was weeping. Limned in the window, she started, almost guiltily, tucking the handkerchief into her small bosom. Jay was uncomfortable. Awkwardly he asked, "Is anything wrong ma'am?"

She rearranged the bun. "I — I look a fright! You see, I came so quickly —"

In spite of her brave performance it must have been a strain. *I have been very insensitive*, he thought. Gently he took her hand. "I am indebted to you, ma'am. I could not have done it without you. Now you must go home and get some sleep."

She smiled a wry smile. "No sleep for me, Doctor! I've got to fix Papa's breakfast. Then I must meet my pupils at the school!"

He went with her to the door.

"If there's anything more I can do —" she offered.

"Not for now. But in the future, if you can see your way clear, I'd like for you to help me when you can."

Shaking his hand almost like a man, she turned away, walking slowly down the street toward the Iredale place. Worthwhile female, he thought; dun and colorless in appearance, perhaps, but you couldn't always tell what was inside the package by the wrapping!

He ate the fried eggs and *frijole* beans Polonius brought. Afterward he sat for a long time before the stove, grateful for warmth. In spite of the rain-washed grime of the windows he could see Mohave City plain enough. There it lay before and around him, the evil

66

town where evil people dwelt. The great mill steamed and smoked, stamps again crashing up and down in pitiless rhythm. Atop the gigantic structure that crawled scabrously up the hill loomed the lion on its scaffolding, Andrew Lamon's golden mark. Down there, by the river, lay Mex Town, a sprawl of tin-roofed shacks and crumbling rain-dark adobe. On the green rise at the other end of town stood Lamon's pillared mansion, built on the sweat and pain of the Mexicans; Flora Lamon lived there. He turned his head slightly. On the muddy bare patch by the reeds of the river was the bandstand where musicians played a long-ago Fourth of July. Long ago? Only six months, but it seemed an eternity.

Closing his eyes, basking in warmth as the old stove creaked and hissed, he relived the scene. *Don't, please — don't! I don't want to die! I didn't do anything! It was Tuck stole the silver!* His face burned, not from the heat of the stove but from shame. Begging basely for his life, he had thrown himself at the feet of the cold-eyed deputy. *Shut up!* That was Tuck, a miserable thief and confidence man, perhaps, but resolute in the face of death. *Don't give them the satisfaction, damn it!* Tuck had thought too, at the last, that he was really going to die.

Into Jay Carmody's mind came small clear pictures, almost photographic images. Redheaded Emmett Dineen and his gavel. The heavy piglike countenance of Monk Griffin, the saloonkeeper. Sarah Iredale's plain anxious face as she pleaded with the court to let the two sinners go. Wagstaff, the deputy "all the way from

Prescott," to keep law and order, with his somber mask and cruel eyes, the easy well-spoken words. The man from the docks — his name was Crisp, George Crisp, in a nautical cap with tarnished gold braid. Hagop Aroutunian, proprietor of the Climax Store, a dark man with a sunken chest that probably meant the consumption. Luke Hodge, from the Star Livery Stable, dry and dusty as his own hay and oats. The blacksmith, a stupid ox of a man, all muscles and no brain — Homer Fox. Billy Dysart, too, the barber at the American Eagle Barbershop next door; the weak man with weak blue eyes and weak chin. Jay saw them again in sharp-drawn images, staring at him as he stood frightened and despairing on the scaffold. He took out the small leather notebook and checked the list of names against his remembrance. Andrew Lamon, of course, had not been present at his humiliation. Apparently he rarely left the big house, preferring to monitor his kingdom through the long brass telescope in his second-floor study. But Jay again remembered Flora Lamon's face as she lounged in the Whitechapel surrey, watching. He remembered the flowered Leghorn hat, bright parasol scepterlike in her hand; the princess of the kingdom of Lamon. Had she smiled, been smiling? Or was that a trick of a disordered mind?

Please, he begged. *Please, I don't want to die!* He heard the metallic scrape as the bar was pulled out and the trap dropped. Everything went black — black until he was aware he lay in the dust beneath the gibbet, severed end of the hangman's rope beside him.

"They cut the rope!" Tuck was incredulous, rubbing his throat. "It *was* a trick! They cut the damned rope near through!"

Unbelieving, Jay crawled to his feet in time to take a rotten potato in the face. A rock hit Tuck on the shoulder and he grabbed Jay. "Let's get out of here, quick!" Together they fled, slipping and falling, trying to shield themselves from the missiles. Catcalling and jeering, the crowd good-humoredly followed, throwing fresh horse apples, clods of dirt, stones, putrid fruits and vegetables, all hoarded for the occasion. One tormentor, screaming with laughter, had a basket of old eggs. Another, waiting in ambush at a turn of the road, emptied a slop jar over them. A fleet-footed stripling thrust a stick between Jay's legs; he stumbled and fell. Tuck jerked him to his feet. "Get up! Run! God damn, I ain't escaped hanging only to be stoned to death!"

They ran and ran until Jay finally sank to his knees. By this time they were out of town, past even Mex Town, fleeing on the rutted wagon road leading to Yuma. The hooting adults had turned back, laughing and joyous, except for one skinny man in a flowered vest and limp black felt hat who threw a last rock and cackled, "Guess *that'll* teach you two boogers a lesson!"

"I can't go any farther!" Jay gasped.

"You got to!" Tuck grabbed his arm, hauling him again to his feet. "They give us this much of a head start, but who knows — that fish-eyed deputy or Red Dineen or someone is apt to give it a second think and come after us with *guns!*"

Jay remained rooted in the road, fists clenched, lip quivering.

"Come *on!*"

"By God, how dare they?"

Tuck turned.

"How dare they trifle with a man's eternal *soul?*"

Tuck slapped him across the mouth. Jay stared at him, one hand groping at his split lip. "You're hysterical as an old woman! They give us a chance — let's take advantage of it!"

"I'll ruin them! By God, I'll ruin them all! You'll see, Tuck! By God, I'll ruin this town and all the people in it!" His voice turned high-pitched, soared. "How *dare* they?"

He stood now before the dirty window, clenched fists raised as he stared at the warped clapboards and false fronts of Mohave City, county of Mohave, Arizona Territory. "How dare they?" he screamed.

The door swung open and Polonius stomped in, rain-wet yellow slicker glistening. He looked curiously about, one finger dredging moisture from his straggling mustaches. "What's all the racket about? Heard someone yelling and I come across to see —"

"Nothing," Jay said. He was wet, too, but with sweat, not rain. His heart pounded like a muffled drum; pulse thudded in his ears. "Nothing at all." He went to the inner door and looked in, then closed it after him. "My patient was a little feverish," he lied. "I gave him a powder, and that put him back to sleep."

CHAPTER
FIVE

In January there were heavy rains. Indifferent to weather, the Papagos and Pimas fished in the river. Indians were poor workers, Andrew Lamon said, and he would not hire them for the mines. Instead they lived in brush huts, subsisting on rabbits, fish, corn, and beans which they grew, and fruits and berries. They appeared happy. It annoyed Lamon, watching through his long brass telescope. Why shouldn't Indians work, and work hard, like everyone else?

Drawing on her riding gloves, Flora sauntered into his office. "Whatever are you scowling about, Father?"

"You're not going riding in this rain?"

She shrugged. "It's just a light mist! And the air is so fresh and clean; the rain washes all the smell of the mill out of the air. You ought to get out once in a while, instead of looking through that old spyglass all the time!"

"Don't turn your nose up at the smell of the mill, my girl! It's what paid to bring you up and educate you and buy you those fancy clothes!"

Flora changed the subject. "What do you think of the new doctor? Jay Carmody?"

"So you call him Jay already! You're getting pretty forward these days!"

She laughed, tossed the wheaten hair tied with a ribbon. "He's very handsome, don't you think?" She was baiting him, which she enjoyed.

"Handsome is as handsome does." Lamon slumped in a leather chair, scratched a match on his thigh to light his cigar. "If you ask me, Carmody's too independent! Got that Mexican boy in the back room of his office instead of sending him packing back to Mex Town! I hear one of the greaser women even had her baby in there the other day. I never hired him to set up a hospital!"

She went to the window. "Emmett's down there. He's going to ride with me this morning."

"Ought to be out at the Vulture instead!" Lamon grumbled. "That troublemaker Rubén what's-his-name — Macías, that's it — Macías made up a petition demanding the cable not be spliced anymore. They demand — think of it! — they *demand* a new cable! Maybe I ought to have Wagstaff put the fear of the Lord into them!"

She bent to kiss his flushed cheek. "You know you have spells when you get angry! Maybe you ought to have Dr. Carmody prescribe some pills for you."

"I don't need pills! All I need is for people to appreciate what I've done for this land instead of causing trouble day after day!" He was still grumbling, drawing heavily on the Cuban cigar, when she hurried down the grand staircase and onto the veranda. The

72

Mexican boy was holding her bay gelding, Emperor, in the graveled roadway.

"There you are," Emmett Dineen said. "By God, I've been waiting long enough! Why do women always say nine when they mean ten?"

He *did* look nice, she thought, in the breeches and riding coat, kerchief knotted about his neck. Still, Emmett generally smelled of the mills. She wished he would use a cologne, but he thought it unmanly.

"Am I truly late? Why, it's only a quarter to ten! And I'm sure I said nine-thirty! So I'm really not late at all. Fifteen minutes is hardly late!"

He drew her by the elbow into the palisade of spike-leaved agaves bordering the house like a medieval wall. "I want to talk to you!"

She looked demurely down, suspecting what he was going to say. Emmett could be tiresome.

"Why is it I don't see you much anymore?"

"You see me now, don't you?"

"Flora, let's not play games! You're always with Wagstaff! Before he came, we used to have good times together. Now he's around you like — like —"

"Like a good friend," she soothed. "And you are my good friend too, Emmett, as is that handsome Dr. Carmody! Why, my goodness — you're jealous!" Lips pouting, she stroked his cheek with a finger. "Poor, poor Emmett! Why do you always —"

Angry, he drew away. "For God's sake, Flora, don't make fun of me! I love you, and I won't be trifled with!" With his whip he slashed savagely at the green

73

swords of the agaves. "You don't know what you do to me when you play with me like this!"

Enjoying herself, she moved softly against him, feeling her body tingle, breasts tighten in the lacy caress of the chemise. This was what she liked; to know men, to seem weak and feminine, yet control them like the innocent brutes they were.

"Emmett, do you *really* love me?"

She gasped, breath almost driven from her as he wrapped her in his arms and pressed his lips against her mouth. Well, perhaps she had miscalculated — a little — but she was still in control. Allowing herself only small pleasure, she waited until he was done and then turned her face away. "Now that was not the act of a gentleman — overwhelming a poor female so!"

Still he held her clasped hard in his arms, rough fabric of the jacket scratching her cheek. She was about to speak again, more firmly this time, when a man's voice made Emmett stiffen; she felt his body grow rigid.

"I'm sorry, Mr. Dineen! And — Miss Flora!" Dr. Carmody, holding the bowler hat in one hand and walking stick in the other, stood at the corner of the house. "I knocked at the door but no one came." His face was impassive. "Ma'am, your father asked to see me this morning. Is he home?"

Flushing, Emmett drew back, smoothing his coat, his red hair. Flora was calm. "Good morning, Doctor! Yes, he's in his office upstairs." She cupped her hand and called. "Amalia! Now where is that woman! Amalia, see Dr. Carmody in! Father wants to talk to him!"

74

Jay bowed, withdrew. The Mexican woman, wiping floury hands on her apron, led him up the stairway. "*Señor! Está aquí el doctor.*" Turning to Jay, she murmured, "*Lo siento mucho, señor, pero —*"

"It's all right," he said. "You were busy, Amalia."

Andrew Lamon slumped in a leather chair, cigar clamped between his teeth, and made entries in an account book. Even though it was morning, the shades were drawn and the room dark. "Oh, it's you, Carmody! I was expecting you. Sit down." He offered Jay a brandy.

"No, thank you, sir," Jay said. "I seldom drink."

Lamon tossed off two fingers in a tumbler, following it with water from a carafe. "Cigar?"

"Don't smoke either, sir — but thank you."

"Model citizen, eh?" Lamon's woolly eyebrows drew together; the mouth twisted in a grimace that might have been a smile. Jay didn't speak, not knowing quite what to say. Apparently he had now been accepted as a proper physician with entree into the town's society, but he remembered to be careful, always careful.

"Been wanting to talk to you," Lamon went on. "Now that you've settled in, I think it's time to establish a few rules."

Jay waited, well-brushed bowler balanced on one knee.

"How do you like it here?" Lamon suddenly demanded.

"Like it, sir?"

Lamon waved. "Mohave City! The mines, the mill, the people!"

Mohave City was the same gray sterile place Jay remembered, the same evil people, the same unwholesome atmosphere. "Well enough," he lied. "Actually, a doctor can practice his medicine anywhere. So long as he is relieving suffering, where he does so is not all that important."

It was a noncommittal reply; Andrew Lamon puffed hard on the cigar. "This week is payday at the mill. You'll get your fifty dollars, like all the other workers." He knocked off an ash. "Making money from your private practice?"

"Usually they don't have any money. But I get along. Some bring a loaf of bread, perhaps a chicken. Others sweep out the office for me — little things like that."

"Who are the sick ones?"

Physicians — real ones, anyway — had a confidential relationship with their patients. Lamon was too curious.

"Well, there's Mr. Aroutunian that owns the Climax Store."

"He doesn't own it," Lamon said. "I do! What's wrong with that Levantine rascal?"

Jay hesitated. "He seems to be pretty far gone with the consumption."

Lamon ground out the cigar. "I notice he's pretty slow getting around. I'll have to hire someone else, I suppose. Who else?"

"The barber. Billy Dysart." Dysart, a weak and foolish man, was afraid he had a sexual disease. It was common knowledge the barber frequently visited Mex Town; his wife had already come tearfully to Jay to ask him if he could do anything about it. Jay had plans for

Billy Dysart. He would play on the barber's fears and drive him mad if he could. "Mrs. Yount," he added. "She's Polonius Yount's wife —"

"I know the old fool," Lamon said. "Polonius, I mean. Helps out at the jail, does handyman work —"

"Yes. Well, Mrs. Yount's heart is a bit irregular. I've been mixing a tonic for her."

"Anyone else?"

"Miss Iredale brought me a Mexican child yesterday. A small boy — Carlitos. Seems he wanted to learn so bad he climbed on the roof to listen to the scholars reciting, and fell and broke his arm. I set it and put it in splints." The job had not been as difficult as Paco Macías. Jay had brought it off neatly and professionally; he was proud.

"That mill hand, the one that fell into the belts. Is he still in that back room of yours? Your 'hospital'?"

Jay shook his head. "I had him carried home. Paco was doing well enough so the family could handle him, though I'm afraid he'll never walk again without a crutch."

Lamon rose, pacing the floor, hands locked behind him. Jay remembered the unhealthy color in the cheeks, the vein pounding heavily in the temple. Perhaps Andrew Lamon also needed medical attention.

"All right," Lamon said. "Well, now —" He paused, looking down at Jay. "Organization, that's what it takes! Rules, reports, authority! You're part of the organization, Doctor, so you must conform. Running a large undertaking like the Lamon interests is not easy. There are important actions to be taken, hard decisions to be made. Recently there has been a rash of mutinies in the mines, at the mill." He waved a hand. "Small mutinies, perhaps — misunderstandings seized on by troublemakers to cripple our production schedules. I have asked Emmett Dineen to take you soon on a trip through the mines so you will be more knowledgeable." He slumped again in the leather chair, lit a new cigar. "Mining is a dangerous business; regrettable, perhaps, but it's fact! So there will be injuries, deaths. You will be called belowground many times, I am sure. And while you are there, treating the injured, removing the dead, comforting the bereaved, you can be of great help to me." Lamon gestured with the cigar. "Dineen is a good superintendent. Emmett knows mining and milling as well as any man in the Territory. But he's — well, he's a rough sort, very hot-tempered. The Mexicans don't like him. He doesn't have their confidence, you see, and so a lot of hanky-panky goes on that I don't know about until it surfaces in a thing like this damned petition the miners got out the other day. You, Doctor, have their confidence! You can talk to them — already I hear they're fond of you! So here's what I want you to do." He spoke slowly, in measured tones. "Keep your eyes and ears open. I want news of what's going on in my mines — what the miners are talking about, who the firebrands are, what trouble they're planning. Do you understand?"

Spy on exploited Mexican miners? Carry tales? Demean the role of the physician Jay was beginning to believe? He was about to give a sharp answer but bit his tongue. After all, he was playing only a role, the role of a physician. He was not in Mohave City to worry about Mexican miners; he was in Mohave City for revenge, pure and simple.

"Yes, sir," he said.

Lamon seemed relieved. "I was afraid," he said, rising to clap Jay on the back, "you were going to give me that old fiddle-faddle about Hippocrates! But I see you know who butters your bread!" Jovial, he led Jay to the door. "After all, I'm an influential man, Dr. Carmody! If you play your cards right this job can turn into something very rewarding!" He stroked his beard, sighed. "Ah, it's hard to get good men anymore! Now you take Emmett Dineen. If Emmett'd keep his mind on things, he'd be a champion! But he's infatuated with my daughter, and doesn't tend to business! Wagstaff, too — I went to the Mohave County sheriff's office myself, all the way to Prescott, to get the best man they had to keep order around here. After all, the Lamon mines are important to the economy of the Arizona Territory! But Wagstaff is turning out to be a disappointment, too." He shook his head. "The man hangs around Flora like a bear around a honeypot!" Lamon grimaced. "A man with a pretty daughter is in for rough weather!" He hesitated. "Used to having her way, you know!"

"Miss Lamon is very beautiful," Jay murmured, not knowing what else to say.

Lamon opened the door, looked keenly at him. "You're not married, Doctor — been married, or anything?"

"Mr. Lamon, I'm dedicated to my work as a physician. Women, to me, are only bodies that sometimes need medicine or surgery. You need not worry."

"Good!" Lamon called after him from the landing. "You and I are bound to get along famously together!"

Jay, a clean man, was in the habit of bathing weekly. This time, after soaping his hair and beard, he saw in the mirror that the dark glossy color had faded; his blondness was reasserting itself. Carefully he brushed Dr. Musgrave's Parisian Tonic and Vivifier into the hair, wondering what he would do when the small bottle of dye ran out.

That day Emmett Dineen was to stop by and pick Jay up for the trip through the Vulture, largest and richest of the company's mines along the river. Waiting for Dineen, Jay got out his harmonica. When Polonius Yount shuffled in to do his morning sweeping-out, Jay — eyes closed in remembrance — was playing "Dreaming Sad and Lonely." Quickly he slipped the battered tin instrument into a pocket.

"What happened to you?"

Polonius's eye was blackened and his mouth was cut. He walked as if he were very tired, and lacked the normal garrulousness.

"Nothing."

"Get into a fight?"

"Not exactly." The old man arched his back and rubbed gently around his lean hips. "I'll scrub the floor today, if you want me, Doc. Looks like it needs it."

Jay was puzzled by Polonius's reticence. "Not unless you feel like it. I can scrub it myself when I get back from the Vulture."

Polonius shook his grizzled head. "No, Doc — I'll do 'er."

Dineen was late. Billy Dysart came in in his barber's apron, followed by Mrs. Hagop Aroutunian and George Crisp, the dock worker. Dysart was secretive, wanting to see the doctor about a private matter. His loose mouth worked, and he was very nervous. Mrs. Aroutunian, a plump dark lady, spoke only broken English, and Jay was not sure what her problem was. George Crisp smelled of bad whiskey. Jay heard the wheels of a rig in the gravel outside and had to tell them, "I'm sorry, but I must go out to the Vulture Mine this morning with Mr. Dineen, the superintendent. If you'll all come back this afternoon, I will hold office hours then."

Dineen was moody. As they drove up the winding road to the works of the Vulture, Jay tried to make conversation.

"Paco Macías is doing well — well, that is, for the accident he suffered. They took him home yesterday."

The superintendent slapped the reins over the backs of the toiling grays, said nothing.

"He'll never walk again without a crutch. Tonight I plan to visit the Macías —" He had remembered that in Spanish it was forbidden to pluralize a family name. They were the Macías. "I've got to tell them — and Paco — the truth. It's going to be difficult."

Jay saw the superintendent was deep in private thought, and let his words trail away into the grinding of the wheels, the plodding of hoofs. But Dineen suddenly brightened.

"There she is! The Vulture! A real glory hole! The vein gets richer and richer the deeper we go!"

They descended in an iron cage for what seemed an eternity. Rocky walls, dripping with moisture and smelling of sulfur, slipped past them in the glow of the candles on the miners' caps. The air turned steamy and warm; by the time they reached the bottom Jay was sweating.

"I remember coal mines back East," he said, tugging at his collar, "but they seemed cool inside — nothing like this!"

"They weren't so deep," Dineen said, with the same pride. "The Vulture is deeper than any mine I know of!" He stepped out of the cage and tugged at a bell rope, signaling the hoist operator above. "Come along!" Fresh white coat already stained with sweat across the back and under the arms, he walked down a Stygian passage.

"Follow me."

In the bowels of the earth, lit only by candles set on brackets and the flaring of torches, Andrew Lamon's Mexicans labored. Sweat-drenched bodies glistened; the air stung with the clamor of picks, the metallic scraping of shovels. Two shining narrow-gauge rails stretched into the darkness, and an iron ore cart pulled by a burro rumbled past. "A lot of mines use mules," Dineen observed, "but a burro eats less, works harder, and is smaller. We can get into some pretty tight spots with the burro carts. That means digging out less overburden to get at the gold."

The miners crouched low, in dark recesses, hacking painfully with short-handled picks and pushing out the stony rubble with bare hands. It was backbreaking toil, and the Mexicans went at it with quiet desperation. Well-drilled teams, knowing what had to be done, they did it without discussion. Anyway, one man could hardly hear the next in the noise.

"Mexicans are the best single-jackers in the world," Dineen shouted in Jay's ear. He pointed to a bare-chested man, booted legs spread wide, who stood before a rocky ledge. In one hand the Mexican held a pointed iron rod and with the other swung a sledge. Quickly the tool sank into the wall as the muscles knotted and bunched with each blow.

"That's Rubén," Jay said. "Rubén Macías. I know him."

Dineen did not appear to hear. "In most mines," he yelled, "they use double-jackers! One man holds the drill and the other swings the sledge! But Mexicans are better! One Mexican can hold the drill and swing the sledge at the same time. That way we save on labor!"

They walked through what Dineen described as crosscuts — tunnels going across the vein for ingress and ventilation, the opposite of a "drift," which followed the rich vein. Their boots sank into slippery clay. "Gumbo!" Dineen growled. "If it wasn't for the damned gumbo, mining wouldn't be so bad!"

From time to time they passed deserted tunnels exhaling foul air. Jay peered in. By the light of his candle he saw funguslike growth hanging down in slimy curtains. Pools of steamy water lay about, and a rat scuttled away from the light.

"Whatever can rats live on down here?"

"Scraps of tortillas, spilled beans!" Dineen wiped his forehead, grinned. "They're Mexican rats! They'll get along!" As they plodded on the pathway of the iron rails, standing back to let an ore cart grind by, he added, "That last was the old September Drift. Richest vein we ever struck, but it finally petered out and we abandoned it."

Ahead there was sudden confusion, shouting, a scattering of the workers. "*Fuego en el agujero!*"

"Fire!" Jay said, alarmed. "He called *fuego* — that's fire!"

Dineen pressed back against the wall, motioning Jay to do likewise. "That's right. Fire in the hole! They're lighting off a fuse. Better put your fingers in your ears!"

A brilliant sheet of light followed by a blast of wind tore at Jay's clothes, sent rubble and dust flying. Jay sneezed, fell into a fit of coughing. Dineen, handkerchief held before nose and mouth, was amused. "You'll learn!" he laughed.

Deeper in the drift Jay saw a mass of rubble. The blast had loosened an overhanging ledge. In the light of torches the ore glistened with veinlike traceries of pure gold. Dineen picked up a chunk, showed it to Jay. "This stuff assays at better than six hundred dollars a ton!" He pointed down a connecting passage where small lights glowed. "That's Hanging Wall Drift. We found a vug down there you wouldn't believe!"

Turning the heavy chunk in his hands, Jay asked, "A what?"

"It's a giant geode — a hollow pocket in the rock! The Hanging Wall vug was actually a room, a big room they broke into." Dineen's eyes glittered. "The walls blazed with millions of gold crystals! The floor was littered with twenty-four-karat flakes big as a thumbnail! There was stuff like spun glass, quartz fibers I guess they were, hanging down in curtains, curtains worked with gold! We took out over a hundred thousand dollars from that one vug!"

Dineen's gaze shifted. He watched a miner shuffle past, pick and shovel over his shoulder, boots smeared with the grayish gumbo. Another went by, then two more. Finally the drift was filled with trudging men going toward the cage. Dineen took a watch from a vest pocket.

"Shift changing." He continued to watch the men. Finally he said, "Got to check them all the time. The bastards'll steal you blind if they get a chance!"

"How do you mean?"

"Why, they try to carry out chunks of ore, nuggets, anything they can hide, and in the damnedest places! When you see a man going off shift kind of nervous, maybe his pocket sags a little too much or whatever —" Dineen stepped up to a miner, slapped the ragged buttocks. Obediently the *minero* stopped, turned out his pocket to show folded tortillas, a rosary, a plug of tobacco. Dineen jerked his head. "Get on with you!"

They followed the off-going shift toward the hoisting cage. As they walked, Jay became aware of a slow current of better-smelling air. He had not realized how foul the atmosphere had become as they went deeper into the drifts. Dineen too drew a long breath. "Ventilating this deep a mine is a problem! The fans are on top at the gallows frame, and not much fresh air gets down this far. But the Mexicans are used to it. Some get a kind of lung fever, but they're the ones that are sickly to begin with."

The drifts and crosscuts were boxed in with what Dineen called "post and cap" timbering, resembling doorframes fashioned from heavy logs. "I hear up in Nevada they're using something new," he commented. "What they call 'square-set' — sort of interlocking cubes, invented by a German named Deidesheimer. But it takes a lot more timber, and good timber's scarce in the desert."

"Back there I heard a creaking from time to time. Is that normal?"

"Timbering always creaks. The Mexicans don't like it — say it's the earth complaining! Can you imagine that?"

As the line thinned out and the cage rose to the surface and came down again, Jay saw Wagstaff, the deputy. Beside him stood Joe Burke, the stocky man with the pepper-and-salt beard Jay remembered from the night when Jorge Macías came to the barred window of the jail. In the flaring light of torches Burke was methodically searching the departing miners.

Pants, shirts, caps, hair, body crevices were roughly examined.

"They can't get away with anything!" Dineen said with pride.

Wagstaff stood at a kind of lectern with an open ledger, checking names. Somber-eyed, impassive, the deputy watched the process, made entries. From time to time he spoke to his helper. "Watch him! That's Alarcón. He's a sneaky one." Seeing Dineen and Jay, he nodded in recognition, went back to his ledger.

"I thought he was a deputy, from Prescott," Jay said. "I mean — he works for the county, doesn't he?"

"Yes."

"Then what's he doing down here?"

"What do you mean?"

"If he's paid by the county, then isn't it illegal for him to be working for Mr. Lamon too?"

"You're damned inquisitive!"

Jay shrugged. "I just wondered."

"So you don't get the wrong idea, this — what's going on here" — Dineen nodded toward the file of miners — "this is maintaining law and order, isn't it? After all, if people are stealing valuables, whether it's salt pork from the Climax Store or chunks of ore from the Vulture, it's breaking the law, isn't it?"

"I suppose so."

"Well, then —" Dineen waved aside a group of miners waiting for the downcoming cage and pushed to the iron-mesh door. "Let's go up! I can't stand the smell of those greasers any longer!"

From the steamy depths of the Vulture they rose into a winter day. Jay, wet with perspiration, hugged himself and shivered. Dineen, slapping the reins over his team, did not seem to mind the change.

"Well, what do you think?" he asked.

"Eh?"

"You were surely thinking about something, the way you're hunched down there, staring at the floorboards."

"About the mine?"

"Yes, of course."

Jay had gone down into the Vulture to familiarize himself with conditions there. The information would assist him in his practice. But in the bowels of the earth he had seen men toiling in unspeakable circumstances; men — even Mexicans were men — oppressed and degraded, forced to burrow like animals. Appalled at the sight, he had briefly forgotten his own humiliation and desire for revenge.

"The mine," he said, "is certainly interesting. And it's obvious that everything is well organized and under control." He went carefully on, trying to sound professional. "I wonder, though, if it's wise to work the men so hard in the heat and boiling water and bad air."

"Let's get this straight, Carmody. You're only a spectator in the mines! Your work is up here, on the surface. What goes on below is my bailiwick. Understand?"

"But I only —"

"I know Mexicans. I know exactly how to work a greaser to get the most ore out of him with minimum expense to the company. You're a professional in your field, I'm a professional in mine. Let's not poach on each other's territory, eh?" The voice was casual but the hard-eyed stare was not.

Jay felt a stirring of resentment. Still, he was practicing deception, and meant to become perfect at it.

"You're right, of course! When it comes to mining, I'm a rank amateur. If I offended you, I'm sorry. Lay it to my inexperience."

They went the rest of the way in silence. Rolling down the hill in the bitter wind, Jay stared at the desert, the gray malignant desert, that shriveled men's minds and souls; the parching sterile desert that made possible the exploitation of the Mexican *mineros*, the warping of the townspeople, the staging of a realistic hanging to drive out anyone who was not similarly perverse.

"Thanks," he said to Dineen, climbing down from the rig.

The superintendent raised his whip. "Anytime!"

Through a rift in the gray clouds the sun shone briefly. Jay stood in River Street before his office. A shaft of late-afternoon gold caught the rearing lion in its spidery scaffolding atop the mill. Like a contaminated stream flowing down from the barren hills, the source of much of the evil in Mohave City could be Andrew Lamon himself — and Flora?

CHAPTER
SIX

Andrew Lamon was not comfortable with raw gold, preferring it in discrete packets, uniform and countable. The government mint was a long way off, so he had had installed in an outbuilding near the main house a steam-powered press to forge pared-off bits of gold into "mint drops" worth ten dollars each. The drops, stamped with a rearing lion and with the Lamon name behind them, were common coin throughout the Territory. Flora, bathing in the ornate flowered Italian tub, was annoyed at the clatter.

"Go tell them to stop that damned noise!" she ordered Luz. "How can I enjoy my bath when that thing is hissing and clanking right under my window?"

Obediently the maid ceased massaging her mistress' neck and shoulders; going to the window, she opened it and shouted down a torrent of Spanish. The press continued to pound.

"*Señorita*," Luz reported, "they say no stop! Your father tell them —"

Angry, Flora jumped naked from the bath and ran to the window. "Damn it — I want them to stop!" Seizing a bottle of scent from her bureau, she hurled it down at the workmen. "Stop, stop, stop! Don't you understand English?"

Someone turned off a valve and the press clattered to a halt. "Mees Flora, your *papá* —"

"I will deal with my *papá*, you ignorant rascal! You may come back later, when I have finished my toilette! Do you understand?"

"Yes, Mees Flora."

Dripping water, she hurried back to the warm embrace of the bath. "Quickly — get another pail of hot water! The things a female has to put up with on the God-forsaken frontier! In Boston we had faucets that ran boiling water! With all Father's money, I don't see why I have to put up with such primitive conditions!"

"Yes, *señorita*," Luz said, and hurried to comply.

Flora relaxed in the warm suds, eyes closed in pleasure as Luz massaged her naked back. James Carmody — Dr. James Carmody — hovered in fancy above her as she lay supine. His hands, the square physicianly hands with the short-cut nails, caressed her shoulders, her throat, her — Feeling the intoxication of his touch, she twisted about in the tub, slowly and luxuriously.

"I hurt you, mees?"

"No, of course not!" Flora's tone was petulant. "But get done, will you? I must go into town this morning and do some errands." Again she tried to relax, feeling the perfumed waters swirl about her stomach, thighs, knees, teasing little eddies and whirlpools that touched her gently as *he* would. But the spell was broken. Jay —

from now on she would call him that, since they were friends — faded from her dream and was gone.

"Bring me a towel!" she snapped.

"*Sí, señorita!*"

As she dried her body she gazed into the pier glass, approving the milk-white shoulders, the narrow waist swelling into full yet not too full hips, the slender columns of thighs, delicately molded ankles and feet. With a towel Luz tried to dry her hair but Flora shook her head impatiently. "Don't touch my hair!" It was her glory; she trusted no one else with the abundant locks, the color of ripe wheat in September.

Lying back on the chaise longue, she did permit Luz to shave her legs. Although it was sometimes painful, it was the latest fashion in Boston society. She liked the sensual silkiness once the golden down had been removed. But the maid, already nervous at her mistress' display of temper, cut a thin red line in the calf of her leg. Flora cried out more in displeasure than pain. "Now look what you've done, you booby! There'll be a scar, there'll certainly be a scar!"

Ineffectually Luz dabbed at the tiny cut, wailing excuses. Flora pushed her away, rose, and threw a pillow. "Get out of here and back to the kitchen! You're not good for anything but peeling potatoes and stoking the range!"

Already the cut had stopped bleeding, but there it was — a blemish on a perfect limb. Perhaps — she smiled — Dr. Carmody would know what to do with it!

Her father was reading the latest Yuma *Sentinel*, brought up the river on the *Cocopah*. Not looking around, he grumbled, "Listen to this — George Tyng's editorial! By God, that man ought to be run out of the Territory!" He read from the editorial. "'Reports have reached us about the continuing exploitation of Mexican miners in the diggings along the river, especially at Dismal Flats, Mohave City, and La Paz. We hold no brief for the Mexicans as such; often they are lazy and ignorant. But they are also human beings, and should be treated as such. After all, since we whites consider ourselves superior, should we not be superior also in pity and compassion for our less fortunate brothers?'" Lamon snorted. "Pity and compassion! Might as well have pity and compassion on jackasses!" Reading on, he said, "'Governor Safford has been informed on the conditions. There is a rumor that he has invested in some of the mines. There is nothing wrong with this. Still, as Governor of the Territory, he should not allow his self-interest to interfere with the tide of sympathy that must arise in the breast of every Christian man who is aware of the deplorable conditions!'" Folding the paper and swatting his thigh, Lamon's face turned red. "By God, if Safford sends any of his lackeys around *my* mines, I'll tell what I know about *him!* He'd better be careful!"

Flora bent to kiss him. He stared.

"What in hell have you got on?"

In stylish riding habit — divided skirt over riding boots, a frilly white blouse under a houndstooth jacket, hair tied up with a ribbon under a long-visored jockey cap she turned, pirouetting. "Like it? I brought the costume from New York."

"Are those — pants?"

"No, of course not. No lady wears —" She made a little face. "Pants!"

"But they look to me like —"

"They're called *culottes*." Spreading her legs wide, she took a fold of the material to show him how what looked like a full skirt was divided down the middle. "*Culottes* are the rage in New York City."

"They're still pants!" he grumbled. "God damn it, Flora, what will people think, seeing you riding around the country looking like a hoyden!"

"They'll think what they already know — that I'm your daughter and do what I want in exactly the same way you do!"

"*That*'s the God's truth!" Still, he looked at her with a grudging approval. "The only thing — I'm surprised you hide your charms under baggy things like that! You never were so modest before. The night we had Carmody here for supper you looked like a whore in that low-cut dress!"

"You liked it too," she retorted.

He turned quickly away, thumbed through papers on his desk. "Riding into town?"

"Yes."

He puffed harder on the stogie. "Going to see Dr. Carmody?"

Of course she had been, but was annoyed. "Why should I see Dr. Carmody? I'm perfectly healthy!"

"Just thought I'd ask. What do you think of him?"

"Why should I even *think* of him?"

"Flora, you can't deceive me; never could! Your mother was the same way — like a pane of glass."

Tired of the fencing, she said, "A pane of glass has little waves in it! Sometimes it distorts things! Maybe you couldn't see through Mother any better than you can see through me!"

"Anyway," he said, "tell Wagstaff I want him to come up here immediately."

"For what reason, pray?"

She was going to discuss his spells but hesitated, wanting to hear his confidences.

"I have information," he told her, "that there's going to be trouble soon in the Vulture. According to my informants, some of the people there have been plotting with agitators from Sonora. I want to warn Wagstaff to be ready for an insurrection." Opening a chamois bag, he poured out a handful of the mint drops, so pure and soft that some stuck together. "To make money a man has to spend money. I intend to have Wagstaff go down to Yuma and round up guns, ammunition — and enough toughs and buckos to handle any trouble that might arise. There — do you understand?"

"I understand," she said. "But it seems — it seems —"

"Seems what?"

"Harsh! Are you sure there's going to be trouble?"

"Not being sure is no excuse for not being prepared!"

"Nevertheless —"

He rose, put an arm around her. She flinched, but his grasp was tight. "You're my daughter, all right!

You're a Lamon down to the ground! There's steel in you, as there is in me! I wanted a son, make no mistake about that! But damn me if you don't sometimes act like a man! I'm proud of you! So don't go female on me about this thing!" Plucking another Cuban cigar from the rosewood box, he lit it. "As long as we keep away outsiders, things run well. We've got heavy commitments, what with the new mines in South America and all the equipment and machinery I've ordered for them, so I — we, I should say — can't take unnecessary risks." He smiled a bleak smile. "We know what to do with troublemakers, don't we? After all, it was your idea to hang those two drifters that wandered in here last year! I watched from the window with my telescope. Never saw two rascals run as fast as they did!"

"They did leave in a rush, didn't they?" She smiled, remembering.

"After you deliver my message to Wagstaff, take this to Carmody," Lamon said. "It's his pay for the month. And tell him I'm getting damned tired of the people he's got laid up in bed in that back room of his! I'm not going to finance his hospital any longer!"

When the stableboy brought Emperor around, she kneed the gelding toward town. But the wind changed, and as she rode a low pall of smoke and fumes crept up the hill. In sudden decision she spurred Emperor away and whipped him up a greasewood-studded ridge, the horse's hoofs scrabbling in loose shale. For a while she sat atop the ridge, looking down at Mohave City, the mill, the mines. Leaden clouds hovered low in the south — probably a storm coming up from the Gulf.

The *Cocopah* was steaming toward the landing; she heard the music of the whistle. Andrew Lamon had invested heavily in the California Steam Navigation Company. Was it possible she would someday own all this? The wealth did not mean too much to her, but power made her tingle, her breath come deep and fast. Still and all, what was power without a man to love her, to adore her, to do her bidding unquestioningly?

Trotting into town, she called out to blind old Don Jaime, sitting on his nail keg before the reed-and-wattle jacal.

"*Señorita!*" Blindly he rose, tattered sombrero held over his clean threadbare shirt.

I must do something for these people, she thought. Her father would be annoyed at such foolishness but she would do it anyway when she had time — perhaps a basket of groceries.

Wagstaff was not at the jail. The old man called Polonius, sweeper-out, part-time cook at the Chinaman's, and general handyman, shook his head. "No, ma'am, he ain't come back from the Vulture yet. I'd advise you to —"

"I'll wait a little while then," she said. But the deputy came in, slapping at his trousers to shake the dust. "Flora!" Taking off his wide-brimmed hat, he smoothed the dark hair into place, ran a finger over neatly trimmed mustaches. To Polonius he said, "Get out, old man! I'll call you if I need you."

Polonius, she noticed, looked battered. That old man, to have been in a fight? To Wagstaff, she said,

"Father asked me to stop by and tell you to come up to see him right away."

"About what?"

She liked Wagstaff — his dark attractiveness, the softness of his voice, even the hint of cruelty in the heavy-lidded eyes. The interesting glint somehow called out to something in her own psyche. But he could be insolent and boorish, in spite of evidence of having been well brought up.

"You'll find that out when you see him, I daresay."

The deputy rounded the desk, glanced through the window at the deserted street outside. "You brought me nothing else but a message, Flora?"

"What else should I bring?"

He looked her over with approval. "Your own delicious self, certainly, and I'm grateful for that! But —" Taking her hand, he drew her near. She smelled maleness, laced with bay rum. With a quick gesture he pulled her to him and planted a kiss on her mouth. The bristles of the mustache stung her lips but she lay limp in his arms, not responding.

"What's the matter? The other night you —"

For answer she raised the riding crop and slapped him across the face, her gray eyes cold and hard. "Nothing happened the the other night!"

"But —"

"If I want you to lay hands on me, I'll tell you first! In the meantime —"

"In the meantime," he said, fingering the weal on his cheek, "I'll wait, Flora. There's plenty of time." He did not seem offended, only amused. "I suppose it's Carmody, isn't it?"

Her face felt hot. She wondered if she had the same tendency toward apoplexy as her father. She would have to be careful to control her emotions.

"What do you mean?"

Laughing, he picked up his hat, carefully recreased the indented crown. "Dineen, me, and now Carmody, eh? What a jolly time you're having! Enjoy yourself, my dear! But let me warn you — things are not always what they seem!"

"Whatever are you talking about?"

"I'm making inquiries about Dr. Carmody. As a friend, Flora, I would advise caution."

"I don't know what you mean," she said stiffly.

He came to the door, stepped out on the porch, untied Emperor's reins and handed them to her. The weal on his cheek had faded. "You know damned well what I mean."

"You're jealous of the doctor!" she said lamely. "You're just plain jealous, that's all!"

On a Saturday morning Jay removed the drains he had put into Paco Macías' leg. The youth, lying on a cornhusk mattress in the Macías adobe, bit his lip but made no sound. "It hurts," Jay said, "but that's the worst of it. The little holes will heal quickly." Stepping back, he wiped his hands on a handkerchief while Paco's father, Uncle Rubén, Paco's mother Filomena, and the dark-eyed sister, Concepción, watched. "I understand you've been walking a little."

Grimacing, Paco sat up. Rubén handed him makeshift crutches, fashioned from tough mesquite that grew along the banks of the river. "*Sí, señor*," Paco admitted. "It hurt, but I walk a little."

"Show me."

Paco tucked crutches under his armpits, hobbled a few steps on the dirt floor with Concepción helping. His face turned white; beads of perspiration stood out on his young brow. The injured leg obviously pained him. He collapsed into a reed chair, gasping.

"That's good for now," Jay said. "Don't force it! It will get better, but I'm afraid —"

They looked at him single-mindedly and he bit his lip. "I'd suggest you lie down again," he said kindly. "Rest will help. And here's something to take when the pain gets too bad." He gave Paco a small vial of the precious tincture of laudanum. His supply was running short. Soon he might have to manage a trip to Yuma on the *Cocopah* for a fresh supply of drugs. Gesturing to the rest of the company, he went into the shabby parlor, out of earshot of Paco and Concepción, who remained with her brother.

"I doubt," he said gravely, "that Paco will ever walk again without his crutches. I have done all I could — it is a miracle, *un milagro*, that he lives. But I am afraid —" He looked around the room with its poor furniture of sleeping pallets, a fireplace of river stones set in sticks and mud, a gaudy colored print of Jesus of Nazareth, *El Señor*, with a guttering candle burning before it. "I am afraid he will always be a cripple."

They were silent, poor people facing tragedy. Filomena's eyes swam with tears. Jorge bowed his head in resignation. Uncle Rubén's eyes were stony.

"But he lives!" Jay said. "That is something to give thanks for! He has not been taken from you!"

Rubén's voice was a deep growl. "We are grateful, *señor doctor*. You are the first man in Mohave City ever to help us! But what kind of a life is that? There is nothing for a Mexican boy to do here but work in the mines. How can Paco work in the mines with crutches?"

Jay put his things into the black bag. There was nothing to say; Rubén was right. Carefully corking the nearly empty laudanum bottle, he realized there might be a score for him to settle on the part of the Mexicans, also. Perhaps this was not entirely a personal vendetta, could not be. But his own revenge would have to come first; the lust for it burned in him like a coal.

"They drive us as if we were animals," Jorge complained. He sat down on a wooden box, hands hanging limply between the patched knees of his *manta* pants. "What use is it to five like an animal?"

Uncle Rubén wiped his mustaches with a big hand. "There are all kinds of animals, *hombre*! Dangerous animals! *El tigre, el oso* — many dangerous animals!"

Jay, fastening the worn brass catch on the valise, said nothing.

"Animals?" Jorge asked.

"Nothing. I — I was just talking." Rubén glanced at Jay. "We talk a lot, *señor doctor*. It is nothing. Just talk!"

Hefting the valise, Jay straightened. "You need not to fear anything from me. What the Lamons are doing to you is wrong, inhuman. If" — uncertain, he paused — "if — if you want to talk about it anymore, send word to me at my office in the town."

They looked at him doubtfully, but with a glimmer of hope.

"I am a *gringo*," he admitted, "but I too have been wronged, and I hate injustice." He put on his hat, nodded. "*Amigos, adios.*"

When he returned, his office was filled with patients. An old Papago woman, hearing of the white medicine man, sat patiently on the bench nursing a swollen hand. Billy Dysart, the barber, paced the floor. Mrs. Aroutunian was there, along with Mrs. Polonius Yount. "Ma needs some more of those powders, Doc," Polonius said, pausing in his sweeping. "She's a dinged sight better, though."

Sarah Iredale, wiping hands on a cloth, hurried through the inner doorway. "I told them you'd be back soon," she said. "They've been very patient."

There was no school on Saturday, and Sarah was free to help out in the makeshift hospital. One of the Mexican miners was near death from what the Mexicans called *fiebre de las piedras*, rock fever, and Jay had had him brought in. It was caused, he was sure, by constant breathing of rock dust from the picks and shovels and giant-powder blasting. There was little Jay could do about it, though if the mines had proper ventilation and water sprays to settle the dust — *Animals*, he thought. *They treat us like animals.* Cattle

102

were valuable, sheep were valuable, even goats were valuable. But Mexicans came cheap.

He carried out his consultations in a corner curtained off with green baize Polonius had cadged from the Climax Store. Billy Dysart was the worst. "So what's wrong with me, Doc?" the barber quavered, wringing his hands. "I know I ain't been no saint, but have I got something — something real bad?"

Remembering Billy's grinning face among the jurors, Jay was exultant at the first real success of his plan. "It's the buboes, Billy," he said, cruelly.

The barber's face paled. "The what?"

"The buboes! An inflammation of the sexual glands in the groin."

Cautiously, Billy felt. "Does seem like there's a little kind of bump! But, Doc, what can I *do?*"

"Stay out of Mex Town!" Jay advised.

Billy swallowed, bowed his head.

Relishing revenge, Jay went on. "In fact, a climate like the Arizona Territory is very bad for you. I'll give you salve for the buboes, but the disease always comes back unless you get to a more temperate climate. Actually, in the last stages it causes a shriveling of the private parts that's pitiful. I guess I've seen a hundred cases!" He shook his head. "Tragic, very tragic!"

The barber was panic-stricken. His voice rose and he clutched Jay's arm. "Where can I go?"

Jay almost felt pity, but hardened his resolve. "I'd recommend someplace like — oh, say, San Francisco."

Billy started to weep. Jay put a hypocritical hand on his shoulder. "Why, man, they must need barbers in San Francisco! When I went to medical school, there were a lot of hairy people there!"

"But all I got is the shop, and a little money saved up! I figured on staying here the rest of my life! How can I afford to go all the way — me and her — to San Francisco!" The barber choked. "Might as well be China!"

"I'm afraid that's your problem, Billy." Jay handed him a small tin. From the "jockeybox" on his trap he had taken axle grease and mixed it with enough asafoetida to make a foul-smelling paste. "Twice a day on the affected parts. That'll be fifty cents."

Pocketing the coin, he felt grim satisfaction. Billy's wife would suffer, too, and he felt a qualm of conscience at the ridiculous diagnosis. But what was the old saying; you couldn't make an omelet without breaking eggs? Thinking of eggs, he was hungry, and remembered the eggs he had hard-boiled the night before, still sitting in their pan on the stove. But the heavy dark Mrs. Hagop Aroutunian demanded his attention, worrying about her husband's night sweats and coughing up blood. He mixed foxglove powders for Polonius's woman, and lanced a boil on the hand of the Papago woman, who tried to give him a lovely turquoise necklace in payment.

Finally, he stepped out of the curtained enclosure and made for the hard-boiled eggs. But someone stepped in the door and called out a greeting.

"Good morning, Doctor!"

It was Flora Lamon, trig and morning-fresh in a riding outfit. The bay gelding he recognized from having seen her riding often in the hills.

"Ma'am, good morning," he said. Sprinkling water from the egg pan on the floor to lay the dust, he said, "I hope you're not ill."

"Not exactly." She took off the hat and shook out her curls. Sun slanting through the open door caught them as they fell about her shoulders in a flood glinting with a thousand fights. "There — that's better! I feel so cooped up with my hair tucked in!"

Sarah was busy with the sick miner. Jay motioned to his visitor to sit down in the single rump-sprung chair, and closed the door. "Ma'am, what brings you to town?"

She handed him an envelope containing mint pieces. "Papa said to give you this; it's your monthly fee. Not much, I suppose, for such a good doctor as you're proving to be! But maybe I can prevail on him to increase it."

He would have been glad of an increase. Most of the townspeople had little money, the Mexicans even less. He had been putting most of his own stipend into buying food for the patients in his hospital. Much, too, he had had to set aside for the eventual renewal of his medical supplies.

"That would be nice," be said, knowing she had something else on her mind.

"I hear Sarah Iredale has been helping you."

"That's right. She's a fine woman. I don't know what I'd do without her."

Her gray eyes narrowed. "She's rather pretty. Or would be if she'd do her hair differently and use a little rouge; perhaps dress in something a little more — colorful!"

"I'm afraid I don't notice those things much, Miss Lamon."

She walked about the room inspecting the bottles on the shelves, the medical books, the rude cot in a corner. "Really, I *am* a patient this morning! Not exactly ill, but certainly in need of medical attention!" Dropping the riding crop, she sat again in the chair. Gracefully she slipped off a boot, pulled down a filmy stocking.

"Ma'am —" he started to say, embarrassed. Then he remembered he was a physician, and had better act like one.

"That damned Luz cut my leg this morning after my bath, and it's *bleeding!*"

All he could see was a thin red line, already healing. She touched it, so quickly he hardly saw; indeed, there was a drop of blood.

"Ah," he said. "Ah, yes." He dabbed at it with a corner of his handkerchief.

Chattily she went on. "I'm not afraid of bleeding to death, but I'm afraid there will be a scar —"

"I hardly think —"

"— and I couldn't *stand* a scar there! Can't you do something, Jay?"

Jay. She called him Jay. He was circumspect. "In a day or two you won't notice it's even there, ma'am. But if you want —"

The wheat-gold hair, smelling of scent, was very close to him as together they bent over the wound. Raising his eyes only slightly, he saw the cleft of her bosom, the ripe fullness below, as her blouse cupped out. His face flushed; the pulse sounded heavy and quick in his ears. Flora's limb was firm and white, a fleshly marble, and the dimpled knee rosy and smelling of womankind. Quickly he pulled himself away from disaster, became professional.

"There are very old remedies for this," he said. "Probably the Greeks and the Romans knew about them." His grandmother, though not Greek or Roman, knew also about egg membranes for cuts, and had often plastered Jay's skinned knees with them. Hands trembling slightly, he picked up an egg from the pan and peeled it; she watched.

"Effective, too," he maundered on.

"Whatever are you doing with that egg?"

Carefully Jay worked the thin white membrane from around the hard-boiled egg, holding a sheet of the gossamer stuff spread between the fingers of one hand.

"Now hold your limb very still."

She watched as he sponged the wound with a little water on a tuft of cotton, then spread the membrane over the thin red line, first pressing the edges of the wound together with his fingers. The translucent membrane stuck tight, almost as if glued.

"There!" he said. "In a day or two it will fall off. I promise you there will not be a scar, ma'am."

He was still bending over her leg, looking reassuringly up at her, when the door to the hospital opened. Sarah Iredale stood there, surprised.

"I'm sorry," she said. "I — I didn't know —"

Awkwardly he got up, wiping his hands with the tuft of cotton. "It's all right," he said, lamely. "Miss Lamon has cut her leg, and I took care of it for her!"

Sarah's face was noncommittal. "When you have time, then —"

"In a moment."

Flora Lamon smiled. It made Jay think of the colored reproduction of the "Mona Lisa" that hung on the wall of the grammar school in Columbus, so long ago. "That was clever of you, Doctor! An eggshell — think of that!"

Was she mocking him? He thought again of the Fourth of July, Flora Lamon sitting in the Whitechapel Surrey. Sarah Iredale, now, was a perfectly predictable female, a standard woman, what people back East called an old-maid schoolteacher.

"I must pay your fee." She made a little face. "Of course, riding — I didn't bring a purse!"

"No matter." He went with her to the door. The dark clouds from the Gulf had brought unseasonable rain. Flora's gelding stood patiently, back wet and shining. Rivulets ran through the mud of River Street, and across the way the Climax Store showed a kerosene lamp against the gloom. "Do you want me to send someone to have you picked up? It's a long ride back to the house on the hill."

She shook her head. "I love to ride in the rain! Emperor likes it too!" Putting on her cap, tucking the hair back in, she paused.

"Ma'am?"

She looked up at him; calculatingly, he thought.

"When you came to Mohave City, I told you the best way to get along with Papa was to do as he wanted. You see, he is very used to having his way." She ran the polished leather of the riding crop slowly through her hand. "People say I am certainly his daughter, that I am of his disposition also. I suppose it is true. Usually I have my way, also."

He did not know what to say.

"I can help you a great deal, Jay," she said. "I hope we will be friends — great friends."

Smiling, she accepted his cupped hands to help her mount Emperor. He still did not know what to say as she rode away, trotting briskly until both she and the handsome gelding were lost in the misty rain. *Flawed*, he remembered, thinking of that night at supper in the Lamon mansion. But flawed — how? He did not know, but Flora Lamon could be a great complication in his plans. Perfect things were predictable; Flora Lamon was not perfect. Thinking of the engine of revenge he was setting on its course, he began to wonder if his vow had been foolhardy.

CHAPTER
SEVEN

"You look so thin and worn, Doctor," Sarah Iredale said. "Here — have more potatoes, and some fried chicken! The town depends so much on you — you must keep up your strength!"

She had invited him to supper, and gratefully he accepted, bringing along a chicken that had been given him in payment for curing a child's croup. His own cooking, along with the greasy stuff brought at times from the Chinaman's, was beginning to sour his stomach; that, and the cumulative strain of the elaborate deception.

"Thank you, ma'am," he said. "You're as good a cook as you are a nurse."

Major Iredale stirred gravy into his potatoes. "You may call her Sarah. 'Ma'am' sounds like one of her scholars at the school."

Sarah blushed, a tinge of color in pale cheeks. "You mustn't mind Papa. He means well. But now I'll get the pie. It's not much, kind of mock-apple made with soda crackers and nutmeg, but it tastes almost like the real thing."

"I'm sure it will be delicious," Jay said. "May I help you?"

In the kitchen she bustled about, putting plates and forks and a pitcher of scarce milk on a tray. "Father lives in a dream world anymore. But I'm grateful he's healthy otherwise, and able to take care of himself."

He watched her pouring coffee. At first he had thought her drab and unattractive, but now he was not sure. Sarah Iredale was fine-boned, her features delicate. The nose was aquiline, brow high, lips and chin firm. He remembered what Flora Lamon had said: *If she'd do her hair differently and use a little rouge; perhaps wear something more colorful.*

"A penny for your thoughts!" she joked.

"Well, I don't — I really didn't —" he stammered.

"I'll bring the coffee in a minute. You talk to Father."

It was a warm night for early spring. Major Iredale lit a cigar and begged to be excused. "I know you, all right," he nodded to Jay. "It'll come to me." He shuffled out to sit in a rocking chair on the porch.

"Papa's so funny sometimes," Sarah smiled. "Maybe it's not so bad to be a little confused when you get old. In his own mind he's happy. He's a young man, riding again with General Lee in Mexico, at Resaca de la Palma. Father got a medal there, from the general's own hand!"

Settling back on the shabby sofa, Jay stretched out his legs. "He's a remarkable man! When I'm his age I don't know if I'll be so well preserved."

She sat across from him, cup and saucer balanced on a knee, one hand adjusting the bun of hair. Idly he wondered how it would look all come down over her shoulders.

"You'll never be his age unless you take better care of yourself!" she warned. "Up all hours tending to people, taking care of them, visiting the mines!" She set the cup down, saying shyly, "You know, your hair has gotten awfully long!"

"Maybe I should have visited Billy Dysart at his barbershop, but since he's left town —"

"Wherever did Mr. Dysart go? It was so sudden."

Jay sipped his coffee. "A health problem. It — it was thought he'd do better in another climate."

"I always cut Papa's hair. Really, I'm rather good at it. If you'd like —"

Her eyes were nice. Not large and heavy-lashed, like Flora's, but brown — clear, and very direct; no female fluttering and batting like other ladies he had known.

"Why, I would thank you for it, ma'am!" Indeed, he did need a haircut. At the hanging it had been very long, and blond. Now he had to keep it short and remember Dr. Musgrave's Parisian Tonic in regular applications. "Where shall I sit?"

In a kitchen chair, dish towel about his shoulders, Sarah cut expertly with a pair of embroidery scissors, blades clacking like a small machine as she trimmed and shaped. A little bolder, she said, "You *may* call me Sarah, if you like! Papa has approved!"

"Sarah, then."

"But I will continue to call you Dr. Carmody. After all, you are a professional man!"

He protested. "But you are a professional too, ma'am — a teacher." He laughed. "Sarah!"

112

Standing back, she inspected her work, handed him a mirror. "Your hair is a little streaked, as if the sun was bleaching it out. But did I do a good job?"

He held up the mirror, slowly turned before the pier glass. "Billy Dysart couldn't have done better!"

As they said goodbye under the sagging vine-covered roof of the porch, Major Iredale's cigar was a glowing coal in the darkness; the old rocking chair squeaked regularly, like the swinging of a pendulum. "Warm for March," the major commented. "Sometimes in Virginia it was like this of a spring night."

"Yes, sir," Jay said.

He shook hands with the major, turned to Sarah Iredale. "I'm most grateful to you and your father for taking pity on a lonely man. Sometimes it's nice to be in a real home, where there's lamplight and a sofa and mock-apple pie — and a woman." Knowing they were in darkness, he took her hand in his; the yellow glow of the parlor lamp did not reach them in the shade of the vines.

"You are most welcome."

On sudden impulse he pulled her hand to his lips. It was warm, and soft.

"Thank you," he said, turning quickly lest she be embarrassed and have to say something foolish. After he had walked quickly down the graveled path, swinging his walking stick, he was uncomfortable that he had been so "forward," as they used to say in the old days.

River Street was deserted. In the moonlight, the only sound was the distant hiss and clamor of the mill. The

American Eagle Barbershop was shuttered. Andrew Lamon was livid at the barber's departure, demanding to know who would now come to the house and shave him each morning. A light burned in the front office of the jail, and shadowy figures moved restlessly about. Over the Climax Store a candle shone in a window where the Aroutunians lived. Jay heard coughing in the stillness, and then a woman's soft voice. Already he had crossed out Billy Dysart's name in his little book; soon he would probably do the same with Hagop Aroutunian. Hagop's consumption had eaten one lung away, and the other was probably tattered as an old lace curtain. In a way, Jay was sorry; not for Hagop Aroutunian, who had voted to hang him, but for the fat Levantine widow-to-be.

On the doorstep of his office, he paused, hearing from the landing below the sound of the *Cocopah*'s whistle. Most of the riverboats did not risk running at night. Captain Thorne was an exception; a lightning pilot, who claimed he could navigate by listening to the river as well as looking at it.

As the lingering echoes of the whistle died away he was aware also of a figure standing in the moonlight before the Star Livery Stable. Casual, booted legs crossed, the man lounged in the shadows with folded arms, face indistinguishable. Jay knew who it was: one of the "deputies" Wagstaff had brought in to stifle discontent among the Mexican miners and mill hands. They were four or five, quiet men with flat hard eyes and a monosyllabic way of talking, the same cruelty in their faces as in the face of Wagstaff himself. Shaking

114

his head, he turned away. Rashly he had blurted something to the Macías brothers about helping them in their struggle. Why was he straying from his real purpose — getting mixed up in miners' grievances, kissing Sarah Iredale's hand in a way that might put ideas in her head, feeling a grudging sympathy for some of the Mohave City people who had once condemned him to hang?

Polonius Yount was in the office, rubbing medicine into his elbow. Starting guiltily when Jay entered, he put the cork back into a bottle.

"Polonius!" Jay greeted him. "What keeps you up so late?"

"Guess I shouldn't have done it, Doc, but you wasn't here and my elbow ached so dinged bad —"

Jay picked up the arnica bottle and put it on the shelf. "Your elbow?"

"It ain't much. Just scraped a little!"

Against Polonius's protests he pulled up the ragged sleeve. The elbow was bruised, skin scraped and bleeding.

"What happened?"

"I — I fell."

Jay frowned. "Seems to me you get banged up quite a lot anymore!"

Polonius shrugged. "You know how it is when a man gets up in years! Falls a lot, stubs his toe — things like that."

Jay dabbed at the scrape with alcohol on a cloth.

"Ouch! That smarts!"

"You're not that old, Polonius."

The old man turned worried eyes on him. "Honest, it ain't nothing, Doc! There's no reason to worry about me. I ain't tryin' to tell you your business, but my advice'd be to just — just —"

"That bastard Wagstaff has been knocking you about. Isn't it true?"

"No! Really, that ain't it, Doc!" His voice trembled. "Like I told you, I just fell down! A kind of a dizzy spell comes on me and —"

"You're not telling the truth." Jay took the old man's shoulder and turned him. "Look at me! Wagstaff treats you pretty rough; I've seen that already. What was it this time?"

Polonius bowed his head. Staring at the floor, he murmured, "The — the window."

"The what?"

"I busted the damned window by his desk when I accidental swung my broom around without looking. There was glass all over his desk when he come in before I could clean it up, and I didn't have time to get over to the Climax and buy a new pane —"

"So he hit you!"

Ashamed, Polonius muttered, "Guess he did."

This wasn't Jay's business either; he would be smart to forget it. Gently he said, "Go home, Polonius. Things may be better soon."

Hopefully the old man looked up. "How better, Doc?"

Jay sighed. "I don't know. But evil sometimes overextends itself, and gets its just reward."

116

There were now three sick people in the makeshift hospital; a similar case of the rock fever, a Welsh foreman from the General Kautz mine with stomach griping and a bloody stool, and a hostler who worked for Mr. Hodge at the Star Livery. A horse had kicked him and broken both legs. There were the day patients, too. An Indian boy had run a thorn into his foot. Mrs. Yount came for a new bottle of heart tonic, bringing the doctor a napkin-wrapped basket of hot biscuits. A Mexican woman with the face of a carved Aztec idol had a female complaint. The sick, the halt, and the lame! When the last one was gone, gratefully bearing away pink pills or paper twists of powders or sometimes simple reassurance, Jay slumped in his chair. A dollar and sixty cents, that was all the cash he had taken in! The patients had, however, left him a string of perch, a chicken tethered by a string to his desk, and a pair of homeknit socks. *The irony of it*, Jay thought; *the destroyer becoming the healer!* Gritting his teeth, he decided he would stop the foolishness. All other things aside, he could hardly run even a bogus hospital on fifty dollars a month.

That night he heard a tapping at a window. With the last fried egg on a biscuit — his hospital patients had eaten soup made from the chicken and the rest of the eggs — he went to the door. In the winter dusk River Street was still and deserted — almost. Across the street the gunman lounged on the porch of the Star Livery.

Going back into the lamplit office, he drew the baize curtains Sarah Iredale had made. Again he heard tapping. He pulled the curtain away from a side window. A dark face stared at him, a man. Carefully he raised the window.

"Jorge? Jorge Macías?"

"*Si, señor. Soy yo!*"

"Come around front, and I'll —"

"No, señor." Hat held across his chest, Paco's father spoke in a hoarse whisper. "They watch. You come, *por favor, señor?*"

Already he was reaching for his black coat, now almost threadbare; the buttons were sound, however, thanks to Sarah Iredale. "Is someone sick?"

"It is only that you said you would help us. We talked, that day — you remember? You said 'My heart is with you.' You said 'Send word to me at my office.'"

"Yes," he said heavily. "I remember."

He recalled also the night in the jail when Jorge had come; he wished he could thank Jorge for that. But now he was Dr. James Carmody. Jorge Macías would not remember talking to a doctor through the bars of the Mohave City jail. "Yes," he repeated. "You go back, *amigo*. I will bring my bag and come in a few minutes, as if I were making a call on a sick child."

Jorge nodded. "*Bueno, señor! Muchísimas gracias!*" Then he was gone, quickly and furtively as before. Cautiously Jay looked out the window, saw no one.

It was a short distance to Mex Town. Carrying his black bag, he walked furtively in the moonlight, shadow long and black in the silvery dust. A mangy dog slunk up, sniffed, padded away. Down the canyon — then two — no, three — doors, turn to the left. He stepped into a puddle of fetid water, and recoiled at the smell of human wastes. The Macías adobe was on the corner, beneath the half-dead cottonwood tree.

Softly he knocked. No answer; only a bony-ribbed cat that pressed against his legs. Dry leaves in the gaunt cottonwood overhead rustled softly. He knocked again. This time the heavy plank door opened to a slit of warm yellow light, against which he could see the wooden bar still in place.

"*Soy yo,*" he said. "*El doctor. He venido para ver a la enferma.* I have come to see the sick woman." This last he said loudly, firmly, in case Wagstaff's bullyboy had followed him.

The black shadow of the bar disappeared and the door opened. "Quick!" a voice said. "*De prisa, señor!*" Then the door was shut and barred behind him. The small room, windows shuttered and airless atmosphere thick with cornhusk cigarillo smoke, was filled with miners, faces lit in shadowed planes. Jay smelled sweat, chilis, candlewax, burning tobacco.

"*Con permiso, señor doctor,*" Rubén Macías said, taking his elbow and guiding him to a seat of honor, a rocker with a mouse-chewed leather seat. "Sit here, if you please."

Eyes becoming accustomed to the guttering candlelight, Jay put down his bag to accept a broken pottery cup. Jorge Macías poured it full of a colorless liquid from a stone jug. "*Pulque,*" he said. "Very good."

The stuff was raw, burning his throat as it went down. Jay sipped it graciously as Rubén, seemingly the spokesman, addressed the group. Jay could make out

119

faces — miners from the General Kautz, the Vulture, and the other diggings, workers from the mill. Paco Macías, rude crutch beside him and bad leg stretched stiffly out, sat in a corner. Sandoval, Herédia, Mejia, Gomez, Cruz, Aleman, Huerta — men, all men — no women, though once he thought he saw Concepción's heart-shaped face peek from behind a makeshift curtain of flour sacks.

Suddenly he heard his name mentioned. He put down the cup, aware that Rubén Macías had been talking about *el doctor. A good man, a kind man. A man who knows us and understands us. He is a gringo but in his heart Mexicano puro* —

"We are proud people, and want to do the necessary things for ourselves. But here in the mines we are slaves, *esclavos impotentes.* We work hard, we suffer, we are paid a pittance, we die like animals, we are buried quick and new slaves take our places!"

There was a murmur of agreement. "*Sí! Justicia! Por todos, justicia!* We must have justice!"

Jorge Macías took the floor. Turning to Jay, he spoke slowly, pronouncing the Spanish words with care. Jay was becoming more fluent, but sometimes the staccato slurred talk of *la gente*, the people, was too much.

"*Señor doctor*, we ask you for help. We are poor people, people without schooling. You know how we are exploited. The timbering in the mines is old and rotten, the air is bad, men are blown apart by bad fuses and giant powder. We are hardly paid enough to eat, so we are always in debt to the Climax Store. The mill is just as bad! Dangerous! Look at our poor Paco! That lion"

120

— Jorge pointed toward the river; Jay knew he meant the golden lion on its scaffolding above the Lamon Mining and Milling Corporation buildings — "that lion is eating us all! Soon there will be nothing left but the bones of us and our children. *Don Diego*, what can we do?"

Don Diego was a term of respect, perhaps of greater stature than *señor doctor*. It meant something almost like "Sir James," and was not conferred lightly.

Jay cleared his throat, embarrassed. "*Señores*, I am only a doctor, a man of medicine. Many times I do not know how even to cure your sicknesses."

"*La fiebre*," someone muttered. "*La fiebre de las rocas!*"

"Yes," he said. "The rock fever. Last week I sat at the bedside of Juan Perez when he died of the fever, and I could do nothing. So I am only a human being too, *un ser humano*, and I do not know the answers to many things."

Rubén, talking around a limp cigarillo, said, "Water brought down from above and sprayed on the rocks after the giant powder blast — that might stop the fever."

Jay shrugged helplessly. "Yes, it would help, but —"

"Did you mention this to *el patrón* — Señor Lamon?"

"He said there was too much water down there already, that they would only have to pump it out." Seeing faces sag, scattered shrugs, despondent looks, he felt miserable. Could he not give them some hope, contribute *something* to this clandestine gathering?

"In Pennsylvania there were coal miners who were maltreated, as all of you are. They mined coal, anthracite coal, not gold."

"Penn-syl-vania?" someone asked. "Where is that?" Someone else puzzled over "anthracite," and Jay did not know the Spanish word but it wasn't important.

"They struck," he said.

They did not understand "struck," either.

"They refused to work," he said. "They stopped working."

There was a chorus of protest. "Then how would we eat? How will we buy *harina de masa* for our tortillas? How will we buy beans, candles, boots to work in?"

"*Señor* Lamon has commitments to meet, debts, large sums of money to pay out. He owes money to bankers in the East who made him loans to buy new gold mines in Peru, in South America, in other countries. If the gold stops —"

"If the gold stops," Paco protested from his corner, "our lives stop! A man can not live without eating!" Awkwardly he struggled to his feet, propped on a crutch. "It does not matter what happens to me anymore! I am not even a man! But those who go down to the mines must eat! So how can you tell them not to work?" Then, ashamed of the outburst, he lowered his head, stared at the beaten earth. "*Dispénseme, señor!* I owe you my life, and I forgot. I did not mean to be disrespectful."

"These men who mined the coal, *el carbon*," a miner demanded. "*Señor*, when they would not work, what happened?"

122

Jay remembered. The Columbus *Dispatch* had run long editorials about "insurrection" in the coalfields. The miners formed a secret union called the "Molly Maguires" to fight company brutality; the mineowners destroyed the union movement with even greater brutality. "It — it did not work," he admitted. "The men who owned the coal mines hired *pistoleros* to beat and kill the miners. So —" He shrugged, frustrated and a little angry. This was not his business; this was not why he had returned to Mohave City!

"*Pistoleros!*" Jorge repeated. "Yes, gunmen! Like the bullies Deputy Wagstaff has hired! They are everywhere, prowling through the mines, stopping innocent people on the streets, insulting, swaggering about, calling us bad names! If we do not work, they will do the same thing to us as they did to our brothers in Penn — syl" — he gave up on the word — "that place, wherever it was. If we had guns —"

There was quick agreement. "It is better to fight than be a slave!"

Jorge went to the door, opened it a crack, listened. Satisfied, he closed it. "I see no one. But they are smart, those *cabrónes*! We can not talk here together much longer or someone will suspect!"

"Guns," Paco mused. "If we had money, we could buy guns! In Yuma, Papa, lives Don Agustín Obledo de Macías, your uncle. He buys guns, sells guns, also shoes and lanterns and harness and potatoes and everything else."

"Money!" Rubén snorted. "If we had money, would we be working in the mines?"

"That gold in the vug," a man wrapped in a sarape said. "It shone, it felt soft and ripe in my hands, like a woman promising many things —"

"And then," Paco cried, "we must give it all to *el patrón*! We hold it for only little while, then it is gone and we are poor as before!"

"If we could only get some out — smuggle it somehow, buy guns —"

There was a chorus of derision. "They kill men for that!"

Jay frowned. "Kill men?"

"Listen!" Rubén said. "Listen, Don Diego! We have tried a lot of ways to take a little bit — such a little bit — of the gold for ourselves. It was not stealing, really, only a way to buy milk for a sick child, or a new pair of boots for those that were worn out and the feet bled on the rocks. But the deputy and his people always found us out. It goes hard with the man that tries to smuggle gold!"

"But — killed?"

Rubén's eyes glittered. "They lock them up in the jail! They beat them till they scream, and make them put their mark on a confession! Then they take them to Prescott, to the court there, to be tried for what is called 'high-grading.'"

"But —"

"Never do they reach Prescott! Always, it is explained, the man tried to escape and the deputy had to shoot him. Always it is that way. 'Too bad,' the deputy says. 'Ah, he left a wife and children! *Muy triste*

— very sad. But you see what happens when a man steals the company's gold!' "

Jay sighed. "It's getting late. I have people in my hospital. Señorita Iredale is caring for them until I return. *Hombres*, I do not know what to tell you. I wish I were wiser —" He remembered to use the correct subjunctive mood. "Maybe something will come to me."

In spite of disappointment they were courteous and respectful. The ragged company doffed hats while Jorge unbarred the door, looked out.

"The way is clear, *señor*," he reported. "*Vaya con Dios, y con nuestra gratitud.*"

Again he walked through the moonlight, alert for watching eyes, but saw no one. Rimming the town, the lights at the gallows frames of the mines flickered in the river mists; twenty-four hours a day, each day, each week, each year, relentlessly following the vein as it snaked through the earth like a golden serpent. Well, he had failed the Mexicans! He was sorry about that, but surely he could not take the whole world's troubles on his shoulders.

Forming vague excuses in his mind, he stopped when he heard a shot from the direction of the General Kautz. Curious, he peered upward. Tiny figures ran about, torches flared, shouts sounded in the distance. What was going on? More shouts, figures running through the scattered greasewood and mesquite. There was cursing as a man fell down a bank in a rumble of gravel; then another shot.

"I seen him!" a voice blared. "He went that way!"

"Which way?"

"Toward the river!"

"I hit him!" someone shouted. "I know damn well I hit him! Look for blood, a trail of blood!"

The shouts continued, grew closer, then diminished as pursuers spread out toward the river. "Maybe in the reeds down there!"

Under the overhang of the Star Livery Jay saw Luke Hodge working late at his books. Luke rose from his high desk and came to join him. "What's going on, Doc?"

"I don't know," Jay said. "They're chasing someone."

After a while the shouts ceased, dying in the distance like a baying of hounds gradually diminished by intervening hills and trees. "Guess they found him," Hodge muttered, and went inside to write again in his ledger.

"I hope not," Jay murmured, his throat tight.

Billy Dysart's empty barbershop turned vacant eyes on the street. Jay's office door was open, yellow lamplight shining across the worn boards of the walk. Feeling melancholy, Jay closed the door and set his valise on the makeshift desk.

"Doctor?"

Sarah Iredale stood in the inner doorway, one hand at her throat. In the other she held a bloodstained rag.

"What is it, ma'am?" He had not yet gotten completely used to "Sarah."

"If you will come here —"

In the rude hospital, sprawled pale and senseless on his examining table, lay a youth no older than Paco

Macías. He had been shot in the back; a bloodstained shirt lay in a heap on the floor.

"He — I think he stole some gold," Sarah faltered. "They shot him! He fell down on the porch, and I managed to drag him in and get him up on the table." She paused, listening. "It sounds like they're coming this way again — the men that are looking for him!"

CHAPTER
EIGHT

Routinely Deputy Wagstaff confiscated knives. To the Mexican workers a knife was a useful tool, carried in a leather sheath at the belt. Occasionally a knifing occurred; someone was injured or killed. But most incidents involved only Mexicans — a nephew became angry at an uncle, two young men came to blows over the same girl, a cuckolded husband took revenge in his own hands. Still, Andrew Lamon did not like his workers to have access to weapons. He had ordered the deputy to seize them wherever found, whether or not there had been a breach of law and order.

Old Pedro Díaz, knife maker since he was a small child in Coahuila, kept on covertly making knives and selling them at reasonable prices. Pedro fashioned knives from files the mill toolroom threw away, from barrel hoops, from worn-out handsaws; there was a continuing supply. Pedro was very old and not able even to double-jack in the mines anymore. Knife making was an ancient and honorable craft that kept Pedro in beans and tortillas. *Qué importa?* What did it matter?

Emmett Dineen, flushed and angry, came into the deputy's office one windy evening and tossed a knife on the desk. "These things keep popping up like weeds! Can't you do something about it?"

Wagstaff took his time, staring idly at the weapon before picking it up. The knife was shiny and sharp, handle covered with thongs braided in an intricate design, leather probably from a cast-off mill belt.

"Where did you get it?"

"That damned Paco Macías! You know — the kid that got caught in the shaker belt a few months ago, the one Carmody fixed up? He came into my office wanting a job, and when I told him he wasn't worth paying anymore, he got insolent and threatening!"

Wagstaff grinned. "You disarmed him, then? A cripple, on crutches?" He put the knife in a drawer with many others.

Dineen's hot eyes stared. "What in hell do you mean by that?"

Wagstaff spoke curtly to Polonius Yount, sweeping the corridor leading to the cells. "Eavesdropping again?"

Polonius chewed faster on a cud of tobacco. "No, *sir!* I was only —"

"Get out!" The deputy jerked his head. "Come back tomorrow and finish!"

"But I was planning on taking the missus on a buggy ride down the river tomorrow. She's been poorly, and I thought —"

"I don't give a damn what you planned! There's too many tongues wagging round town, and yours is hinged in the middle and flaps both ways!"

Polonius stood the broom in a corner, wiped hands on the seat of tattered pants. "Yes, sir! Don't want to cause no trouble! I'll be back later, Mr. Wagstaff."

In a way Dineen admired Wagstaff's glacial coolness, the way he never had to raise his voice, the fact that he never seemed to sweat, even in extreme circumstances. Too, the deputy was obviously respected by the gunmen he had brought to Mohave City. Dineen knew one or two by reputation, and they were killers. But he was not about to have his own bravery questioned.

"What you said about Paco — was that a comment on my courage, then?"

Wagstaff laughed, took out his hunting-case watch, looked at it "Leave the knives to me, Dineen! You run your mill and your mines, I'll take care of law and order!" But he could not resist a final gibe. "Seen Miss Flora lately?" He knew full well Flora was tiring of Emmett Dineen. In fact, she had told him so.

"No, I haven't seen her lately, because you've been sucking around behind my back, telling lies!"

Wagstaff stubbed out the half-smoked cheroot, leaned back in the chair with hands clasped behind his head. "I don't have to tell her any lies about you, Dineen. Your character speaks for itself. Flora knows you want her just for the mill and the mines when the old man dies."

"That's a lie! I love Flora! Love is something a cold-blooded scoundrel like you doesn't know anything about!"

Wagstaff smiled, a tightening of lips over even-set teeth. "Temper, Dineen! Temper!"

Dineen pointed an orange-furred finger. "Anyway, what could you ever offer her? A hired man brought in from Prescott to do a trifling job you can't handle! There's dozens of peace officers in the Territory that'd be glad to do a proper job for less pay." Face flushed, he pounded on Wagstaff's desk. "Besides, you're taking money on the side from old Lamon! You're paid by the county to do a *job* for the county, and any other remuneration is illegal — I looked it up!"

Wagstaff's calm was intact. Puffing his cheroot, he locked hands behind his head. "You're going to get an apoplexy!"

Breathing hard, Dineen glowered at him. Never had he hated a man so. The dislike was compounded by the fact that the deputy was treating him like a child. Confused and unnerved, he could only splutter, make nonsense sounds.

"What was that?" Wagstaff asked abruptly, holding up a finger.

"What? What in hell are you talking about, damn it?"

"Keep your flannel mouth shut for a minute, will you?"

From the hills above came distant shouts, the sound of firearms. The shouts grew louder. There was more gunfire. The deputy went to the window, stared into the night. "Looks like trouble at the Vulture."

"I'm not surprised," Dineen said, almost good-humoredly. He went to the door. "That's your business, Deputy! If you can't handle it, just let me know!"

131

Wagstaff reached into a drawer and pulled out a Colt's revolver. Dineen watched him, uncertain, but the deputy stuck the gun into the waistband of his trousers. "I've always had a good memory," Wagstaff said. "No man has yet talked like you talked to me and got away with it."

Dineen turned on his heel. As he passed through the door a man brushed by him in a gust of sand-laden wind. The superintendent recognized him; a tough from Castle Dome City who was reputed to have killed three others in a single draw-poker disagreement. His name was Singer.

Frustrated, Singer paused to catch his breath. "He got away!"

"Who got away?" Wagstaff demanded.

Singer's chest heaved. "He — this greaser! The shift was going off at the Vulture, and he tried to smuggle out a big nugget, a nugget the size of your fist! The cage was just going up and he broke and ran for it. The damn Mexicans just gathered around him and we couldn't even get at him! By the time we got to the top he was dodging toward the river! I took a shot at him when I seen him wading through the rushes!"

Wagstaff walked out into the night. Across the street Dr. Carmody's sign swung creaking in the darkness. The new doctor stood in the doorway, outlined in the yellow glow from the lamp within.

"You don't need to look any farther, Deputy," Dr. Carmody said. "The man — he's a boy, really — is in here."

Having run down their quarry the rest of the pack, all hard-bitten faces and drawn guns, gathered around Wagstaff, waiting for him to take custody.

"You want to bring him out?" Wagstaff asked. "Or shall I come in and get him?"

Dr. Carmody's face was invisible in the darkness; he was only a silhouette. "I'm not in favor of either," he said. "The boy is badly wounded. After I've treated him, I'll be in touch with you."

There was stirring behind the deputy, muttered comments.

"I want him now!" Wagstaff insisted.

"You can't have him now."

"I'm going to put him in a cell!"

"He'll die there — and quickly."

Wagstaff made an impatient gesture. "That's neither here nor there! He's a thief. I've got to take him to Prescott to stand trial."

Dr. Carmody was stubborn. "When he's well enough you can take him. But I warn you it will be a long time, if ever, before he can travel. If he gets to the stage where he can sit up in a chair, perhaps you can try him here."

The deputy spoke cautiously. "Try him here?"

"I understand that has been done on occasion. You hanged two harmless drifters who had the temerity to visit your city."

Wagstaff's eyes narrowed. More cautious, he murmured, "This is a crime against Mohave County, not a municipal offense."

A woman's voice spoke behind Dr. Carmody. "He's bleeding badly, Doctor! Can't you come?"

"Damn this palaver!" Singer grumbled. "Wag, let's go in there and drag the greaser out! The sawbones ain't going to stop us!"

Dr. Carmody started to close the door against them but Wagstaff stepped on the porch, put his foot in the way. "All right, then — but I'm going to watch while you do whatever you do."

"I don't want a lot of people crowding around. It's — it's serious surgery, and hard enough to bring off even without any interference!"

The deputy stepped inside, tipped his hat to Miss Sarah Iredale. Her eyes were wide and frightened, and she held a bloodstained cloth. To Dr. Carmody he said, "There won't be a lot of people. Just me. And I won't interfere — right now, that is."

Dr. Carmody shrugged. His face also, Wagstaff thought, looked pale and drawn — odd, for an experienced surgeon.

"All right. I guess I can't object to that."

Sarah Iredale started to say something, but Dr. Carmody brushed her away, impatient. "We've got to hurry and stop that bleeding!"

With the deputy watching from the shadows beyond the reach of the lamp hanging over the makeshift table, the two rolled the youth over on his back, pulled off his clothes. He had been shot with a weapon of large caliber. Where the ball had emerged was a gaping wound looking like some horrible flower, with petals of mangled flesh. The sheet covering the table was wet

134

with blood, and from the sodden hem blood dripped on the floor.

"He stole a nugget," Wagstaff said from the shadows. "Did he have it on him?"

Jay picked up a scalpel and stared helplessly at the wound. The boy was no more than eighteen; body slim and perfectly formed; legs straight and well muscled, shoulders broad, bared chest almost hairless. Like a bronze statue the form lay, complete and masterfully sculptured — except for the horrible wound.

"One of old Pedro Díaz's grandsons," Wagstaff said, casually. "I know him."

The hand with the scalpel trembled, and Jay moved about so his back was to Wagstaff, not wanting him to see. Nothing in studying for his role as a doctor had prepared him for this! A broken leg, a faltering heart, an arm slashed by a knife — these constituted no real problem; some carpenter work, a little foxglove powder, a needle and thread — they sufficed. But this! He had been playing God, and now God had caught him at it!

"What about the nugget?" the deputy asked.

In an agony of indecision Jay dropped the scalpel, took the rag from Sarah, and pressed it against the ragged wound. The flow of blood already was dwindling, and finally it stopped. He flung down the cloth and pressed his ear to the brown chest. Nothing — no sound. He lifted, the limp wrist, feeling for a pulse. Nothing.

"He's dead," he murmured.

For a moment the room was silent, the only sound the creaking of his sign outside, J. B. CARMODY —

PHYSICION AND SIRGEON. Mortally wounded, a boy had staggered into his office, and the counterfeit doctor had failed him.

"Dead?" Sarah asked, knuckles to her lips.

He nodded, drawing the dangling ends of the bloodstained sheet over the still form.

"There!" he said to Wagstaff. "Take your damned pound of flesh!"

"I ask you again, under penalty of law!" the deputy insisted. "Did he have the nugget on him?"

Dr. Carmody sat in a sagging chair, pressed fingers against his temples. "Miss Iredale and I undressed the boy to prepare him for surgery. I saw nothing of any nugget. Perhaps he dropped it in the reeds along the river."

"As a doctor, a professional man, you'll swear to that?" Jay, looking up dazedly, saw that the saturnine face seemed grimly amused.

"I don't believe in oaths," he said wearily, "other than that of Hippocrates. But I do not lie, if that's what you mean."

"If you find the nugget, then, I guess you'll let me know."

Jay remained sitting motionless in the chair as the door closed. Now that the shock had alleviated, sweat beaded his forehead; his heart pounded.

Sarah Iredale came close. "Doctor, I wanted to tell you that —"

Wearily he waved his hand. "Not now, Sarah. Please! I — I've got to collect my thoughts."

136

Why had he spoken of the hanging to Wagstaff? The deputy was a shrewd man; taunting him only made his case the more perilous. But Jay had been rash, proud, and could not resist the opportunity. Pride, that was it — what the old Greeks called *hubris*; "overweening arrogance." Too, that lofty talk about the Hippocratic oath! Though he knew the gist of it, he was not even certain of the wording.

Sarah still stood beside him. He reached out and took her hand in his, wanting — needing — comfort. What a fool he had been! Since coming to Mohave City he had slipped into a way of regarding himself as a *real* doctor, with knowledge and skill to relieve suffering, save lives. That foolish belief had betrayed him. A proper doctor might have done something for Pedro Díaz's grandson, might have cured Hagop Aroutunian, might have brought the hope of modern medicine to this isolated mining town. But he — Jay Carmody — was a curse on them, an impostor!

"I killed him!" he blurted.

Sarah knelt beside him. Misunderstanding, she said, "You mustn't say that! You could have done nothing — Jay. The boy was dying when he staggered into your office!"

"I could have done something!" In spite of himself he began to weep. "By God, I *should* have done something!"

She did not know what he really meant, that if he had been a proper doctor —

"Don't talk that way anymore — please." She put a finger to his lips. "You're distraught, and tired. You take things too hard!"

Her reassuring touch, her nearness, overcame him. The shame of the hanging, the months of deception, living a lie — all drained his strength. Sarah, still not knowing, put her arms chastely about him, a mother comforting a child.

"Death is a tragedy to us here on earth, but maybe the boy has gone to a better place. You did all you could do, all any doctor could do!"

How he longed to confess, to tell her everything! But he couldn't; he was alone, and would have to remain that way. In the effort to compose himself he bit at his lip until he tasted salty blood. When she handed him a handkerchief he thrust it away, then immediately apologized, "I didn't mean that! I'm grateful for you, Sarah — for your help, and understanding. I — really, I don't know what I'd do without you." Taking a deep breath, he got unsteadily to his feet. "I must find old Pedro and the family and tell them about — about —" He gestured toward the sheet-draped form. "You're not afraid? I mean, staying here with him till I get back?"

"No, of course not! But I will pray for him, wherever he is now."

Feeling some of the tension leave him, he smiled. "I thank you, Sarah. You are a fine lady."

They never found the big nugget. Wagstaff had his people out for days, searching, until they were sunburned and leg-weary. Through the window Jay watched them comb the greasewood-studded hills in unseasonable spring heat; it was the Mexican Easter season. There was no church for the Mexicans, no

138

padre — Andrew Lamon disliked the Catholic Church. "Gets them stirred up," he objected.

From the window Jay turned to Mr. and Mrs. Aroutunian. They sat stiffly together on the sofa as if posed for a portrait, two figures in what were probably their best clothes for the visit to the doctor; the merchant in a fuzzy gray suit with a stiff collar and new boots, Mrs. Aroutunian fat and anxious-faced in a too-tight Basque jacket and flowered straw hat. Aroutunian showed no emotion but patient resignation, from time to time coughing into his handkerchief.

"I'm sorry," Jay said. He had been staring out the window in an effort to find the right words, but there were no right words. The death of old Pedro's grandson had shaken him to his core. Things would never be the same. "I'm sorry," he started again. "There is nothing I can do. At this stage, with so much blood coming up, it is only a matter of time. I — I can perhaps make Mr. Aroutunian a little more comfortable, but —"

He broke off, looking out the window again to quiet his emotions.

"There be no hope at all?" Mrs. Aroutunian asked, hands white around the knuckles as she clasped the handle of her reticule.

Jay was certain the pity he felt was not for Hagop Aroutunian, but for the poor fat soon-to-be widow. "Well, I suppose there is always hope. In medical history there are cases of spontaneous remissions." Seeing the puzzled look on her face, he tried again.

"Cases where people recovered — let us say — miraculously. But such cases are few."

Aroutunian rose, hat in hands, face pale under the Mediterranean olive. "Come, Mamá! We don't take any more of the doctor's time! He has sick people."

"But —" Her prim mouth worked convulsively.

"No." The storekeeper took her hand. "Come!"

At the door he paused, a shabby figure with bent shoulders and delicate hands. "We will be all right, Doctor — Mamá and me. And we know you try help us." Averting his face, he groped blindly for Jay's hand. "You are good doctor, sir. You are — you are something new for this place, this town."

More moved than he cared to admit, Jay watched them leave. Had he so misjudged people? No, there were real rascals still! But he was uncomfortable, the more so when the porcine Monk Griffin, the barkeep at the Empire Saloon, came in with a mashed finger sustained when a beer keg pinched it. While Jay cut away the dead flesh and bandaged the finger, Monk talked in a meandering fashion.

"I don't let them in the Empire. Never did! Mr. Dineen's instructions!"

Jay, in a brown study, split the end of the bandage with his scissors and tied a knot.

"Sometimes I wonder, though, if it wouldn't be better to let them have a schooner of beer or a shot of whiskey instead of getting drunk on that stinking juice they make out of maguey cactus — they call it *pulque*."

Jay folded the scissors, put them in his valise. "I guess I wasn't listening. Who? I mean — who is it better to —"

"The greasers," Monk explained. "I was talking about the miners. Any man, Mex or not, is the better for a little snort of whiskey once in a while. I was just saying — it wasn't my idea to keep them out of the Empire." He held up the bandaged finger, stared at it thoughtfully. "I guess they drink to forget, like the rest of us does."

It was a surprisingly sensitive thought on Monk's part; Jay had never credited the man with perceptiveness.

"It's a hard life, down in the mines," Monk went on. "There ain't no one deserves that kind of life, even greasers!" He rose, took out a dollar bill.

"My fee is only fifty cents," Jay said. "I'm afraid I haven't got any change."

"Keep it, Doc! Maybe one of them old Papago ladies that comes in here can use money for their medicines." At the door Monk paused, rubbing an unshaven chin. Then, almost conspiratorially, he closed the door, approached Jay again.

"There's something I want to tell you."

Jay waited. Griffin scratched his privates, seeming uncertain how to start. Jay tried to help.

"Is it — a social disease?"

Surprisingly, the barkeep blushed. "Hell no, it ain't anything like that, Doc! I got me a good woman, and I ain't no roamer!" He spat on the earthen floor. "God damn it, I didn't mean to do that either! Sometimes I ain't got the manners of a yellow cur dog!"

"That's all right," Jay said. "What is it, then?"

"You — you be careful," Monk stammered. "I mean — well, there's talk going round."

"What kind of talk?"

"Well, I can't hardly put my finger on it, exactly. But little things drops here and there. People comes into the Empire and talks, maybe talks too much when they've had a snootful. Some people don't —" Griffin paused, clawed at his stubbled chin in an agony of embarrassment. Finally he blurted, "They say you ain't what you seem to be!"

"Who says that, Monk?"

"I might be in trouble for speaking it out loud, but it's — it's — Mr. Dineen, the superintendent."

Jay was becoming expert at dissembling. He chose his words carefully. "I — I'm only a man who tries to help people. Everyone knows that."

Monk held up the bandaged finger. "Feels better already! *I* ain't got no doubts." He opened the door again. "Doc, I got to go! No one can't buy beer when the front door of the Empire is locked!" He left Jay staring at the paper dollar, and wondering.

The foreman from the General Kautz mine was cured of his bloody stool by tincture of belladonna, and the hostler with the broken legs now sat sunning himself in a chair before Hodge's livery stable. Hodge, unaccountably, was paying him a small salary while he convalesced. The merchant even donated old boards and rusted tin roofing to add a hospital "annex," and

142

Homer Fox, the blacksmith, made hardware, hung doors, and painted.

But with the additional space there was still crowding. A widow brought her little boy with a forbidding canker on his leg. There were the usual casualties from the mines and the mill. An old *curandera* — a Mexican woman rumored to be a witch — was brought in with a growth in her nose that made it almost impossible for her to breathe. Her own medicines had failed, and sheepishly — she was a good-natured, broad-faced woman — she asked for help from another practitioner. Jay cut it out, and although old María bled a great deal, the wound healed quickly and normal breathing was restored. Singing his praises, referring always to Jay as *el gran maestro* — the great master — she remained to assist at childbirths, which Jay never relished, and supplementing his own diminishing stock of medicines and drugs with her own herbals, seeds, and roots and berries ground in a mortar. At first Jay had been hesitant. Now there was no doubt in his mind of their efficacy — at least, the efficacy of some.

But there was always the matter of money. Sarah Iredale helped as much as she could from her meager salary, and the citizens of Mohave City paid what they could — which was little. The Mexicans had even less cash, but brought him beans and tortillas, sometimes meat from a freshly slaughtered goat, or venison from a deer that had strayed too near Mex Town. The Indians came also, silent and wary, but bringing fish from the river, along with the corn and beans they grew on

143

scanty plots. But cash was what he needed — cash to buy medical supplies! Little was forthcoming.

One day he was emptying a slop jar back of the hospital when Luz, Flora Lamon's maid, brought him a perfumed note in a lion-embossed envelope of finest parchment paper. While the maid waited, eyes respectfully downcast, he read it:

Dear Jay:

Father is very ill, though he will not admit to it. He remains in bed, fretting and fuming, and complains there is no strength in his arm and leg. He has forbidden me to call you, and is determined he will overcome by sheer will. Still, I believe he needs medical attention. Can you come — for me?

Flora

Too weary to walk, he asked old María's grandson to harness up the mare and bring the trap around. Luis insisted on driving him and Luz up the hill to the Lamon mansion, sitting high on the seat with whip held proudly aloft.

Carrying his walking stick and the black satchel, now almost empty, Jay walked up the high steps between the tall columns. Luz departed to tell Flora. Uneasy, she returned to guide him directly to the bedroom of the *patron*. Flora was nowhere in sight.

"Heard you drive up," Andrew Lamon grumbled. He was propped on pillows in a four-postered bed. "Who the hell asked you to come here?"

144

Jay sat without invitation. "I heard you were ill." Automatically he felt for a pulse, but Lamon drew his hand away.

"There's nothing wrong with me! It was Flora, wasn't it? Flora sent for you, behind my back!"

"Give me your other hand," Jay said.

"Why?"

"Can't do it, can you?"

Lamon cursed. "It's gone back on me! But I'm not worried. It's happened before. After a while it gets all right again." Beard untrimmed, dark circles under eyes, he glowered. "It's a wonder a man has his health at all, what with the worries and responsibilities I've got! And you, Carmody — where the hell are those reports I keep asking you to make on the Mexican troublemakers?"

Jay was silent, pouring the last of his diuretic powders into a paper twist.

"Damned rebellious scoundrels — thieves stealing me blind! Then, Eastern bankers wanting more and more interest on their money, the Peru thing touch-and-go!" Lamon's face was flushed. He leaned over to hawk into a brass cuspidor. "Damned daughter of mine, too, flibbertigibbeting all over the place, Wagstaff and Dineen fighting like hyenas —"

Jay gestured to Luz, standing uncertainly in the doorway. "Bring me a glass of water, please."

"I need them both," Lamon went on, voice rising. "God damn it, I need them both! But I never counted on them stalking Flora the way they do!" He gritted his teeth. "Flora's man-crazy! That's a hard thing for a man to say about his daughter, but it's the truth; she'll chase anything in pants! Don't tell me — I had her watched while she was in Boston!"

Luz did not bring the water; Flora did. In China silk wrapper and embroidered sandals she said to Jay, "I didn't know you were here. I'm sorry."

Andrew Lamon stared. "Go and put some proper clothes on!"

She ignored him. "What was the water for?"

Jay held up the twist of paper. "Give your father this, please, stirred into the water."

Furious, Andrew Lamon knocked the paper from Jay's hand; white powder spilled on the carpeting. "The hell she will! I don't need medicine! All I need is a little time to get on my feet!"

"God damn it!" Jay blurted. "That was the last I had! I'm almost out of everything!"

"You're a problem, Father," Flora sighed. Undoing the ribbon that held back her hair, she tossed the curls about her shoulders, wearily rubbing the nape of her neck. "Whatever shall I do with him?"

Jay rose, picked up the valise. "Mr. Lamon," he said stiffly, "you're ill, and need attention. But if you won't take the medicine I prescribe, that certainly is your privilege." He hesitated. "I — at this time — I mean, I didn't want to bring it up while you are indisposed. But I must tell you that I don't have enough money to keep on the way I have. Fifty dollars a month is very little. What I get from the townspeople and the miners is not enough to buy medical supplies and keep the hospital running. I wonder, could you see your way clear to —

to make some funds available to — to —" With Lamon glaring at him, it was difficult. "I need more money to do a proper job," he managed finally.

Lamon snorted. "Fifty dollars a month is plenty! Anyway, I never told you to treat Indians, to start a damned hospital, build a refuge for every loafer and malingerer in town! Money is scarce! I need every ounce of gold out of the mines just to pay interest on the loans!"

"But —"

"Out of the question!" Lamon waved his good hand in dismissal. "Now get out of here and let me have my rest! I've got books to balance, letters to write, things to do!" He looked at Flora. "You too, you scheming female! What was it old Shakespeare said? 'How sharper than a serpent's tooth it is to have a scheming daughter'?" He turned his face away, lay back on the pillow.

Flora put a finger to her lips, gestured to Jay. In the hallway outside Luz hovered; Flora sent her away.

"I'm sorry," Jay muttered. "Truly sorry! But I can't help him if he doesn't want help!"

"Come with me." Flora led him down the hallway to the bedrooms, her slippered feet making a soft brushing against the Turkey carpet. At the end of the hall, beside a potted palm in a brass urn, she paused. "I want to talk to you."

"About what, ma'am?"

She opened a door. "You know my name! It is not ma'am — it is Flora!"

The walls of her room glowed with rich brocades. Tasseled pillows were piled in every corner. The chamber was fragrant with musky scent from incense smoldering in a brass Buddha. In the middle, almost like a throne, was an immense bed; not a bed, really, but more of an Oriental couch. The richly worked coverlet draped downward in elegant folds. Carefully Flora closed the door, and smiled at him.

Nervous, Jay fumbled with the black bag. "You wanted to talk to me, you said."

While he stood awkwardly in the entryway, perspiration beading his forehead, she sat on the bed, slippered feet crossed so he could see delicately molded ankles.

"You must come nearer." She patted a pillow. "Sit here."

He did not like the way he was feeling. This was only a way to betray himself. Cautiously he sank down on a pile of pillows, almost a divan.

"There! Isn't that better?"

"Really, I must go! I have patients who are waiting!"

"Then they must *be* patient, must they not, as I have been for the past several months!" She laughed at the little joke, tongue darting round the red circle of her amused mouth.

With an effort of will he crossed his hands professionally over the black bag. "I suppose so — Flora. But what are we to talk about?"

Casually she clasped a knee in her hands, raising her limb so that there was a flash of pale thigh. "You need money, I know that! As a female who is of a business

148

turn of mind in *spite* of what Father thinks, I recognize a good job when I see one being done. Therefore I will help you, Jay. I have money of my own. I will give you whatever you need. I know you are honest, and will not try to gull me."

"That is a kind offer. But a person familiar with business should know also that offers are not usually made out of kindness."

She leaned toward him, her breath clear and sweet, like a child's. Breasts swelled richly out under the silken restraint of the robe. "Father told me you were wedded to your practice, that you were not interested in that gentle commerce between male and female. Is that true?"

She was mocking him, and he tried to restrain himself, feeling resentment mingled with physical attraction; both powerful emotions.

"You made me an offer, ma'am," he said. "What do you expect in return?"

Rising, she parted the Chinese robe to stand before him in a diaphanous gown through which he could see the outline of her body, all female and welcoming; now she was not mocking him. "If you want," she said, voice meaningful with passion, "you may seal the bargain now — Jay."

CHAPTER
NINE

Jay was stunned. A feeling of unreality gripped him; unreality, passion — and caution. Here, in this house, almost within earshot of Andrew Lamon's room?

"Well?" Flora smiled, sure of herself, lips moistly parted, body disposed with one slender leg advanced, rounded arms gracefully holding aside the robe.

Attracted yet wary, carrying out the action as if by timed and deliberate instruction to each joint and muscle, he rose, remembering what Flora Lamon had said about her father. *The best way to get along with him is to do what he asks.* In her he had already seen much of her father.

"There is no doubt you are beautiful," he murmured. "In fact, you are the most beautiful thing I have seen for a long time!"

Regarding him steadily, she held the pose. A narrowing of her long-lashed eyes betrayed impatience, perhaps a small displeasure. "I do not need you to tell me that!"

"Beautiful," he temporized, "yet hardly attainable, ma'am, by a poor physician. After all, your father hired me, and I depend on his goodwill."

The filmy Chinese silk trembled as she held it wide. "What is all this talk about goodwill?"

"I merely spoke —"

"Indeed, you spoke! You are still speaking!" Flora dropped the folds of silk, shook her head impatiently; the wheaten hair swirled about white shoulders. "I know men, and I know you, Jay!" She held out her arms. "Come!"

He wavered, and hoped she did not notice. "I am a physician, and have taken an oath to —"

"Damn it, Jay — stop talking! You — you are demeaning me! I am not one to beg, you should know that!" The full lips trembled; her eyes began to dim with tears. Still holding out her arms, she repeated, "Come! That is all you have to do!"

"Flora —" he stammered. "Flora, I — I —" He could not find the proper words.

"Come!"

Yearning for him, still holding out her arms, she managed a tremulous smile through the tears. But the smile only brought him the memory of that day on the gallows. *Through the small end of the telescope she was smiling at him. The lady in the Whitechapel surrey, the lady watching, wheat-yellow hair spilling out from the Leghorn hat, parasol aloft.*

"Please — Jay."

Her weakness gave him a modicum of strength. *The Lamons*, he thought, *that was where the evil had come from*. The Lamons were used to getting what they wanted, and would not be denied.

"Flora," he began again, "I can't —"

He was unprepared for the tigresslike rush. Her nails ripped his cheek, the soft impact of her body sent him tumbling. A bronze lamp overturned, a mirror broke, a bottle of French perfume lay on its side and the room filled with musky scent.

"You — you eunuch! You —"

Struggling to his feet, he grasped the flailing arm. "Please, Flora —"

"No man has treated me so! I will not have it!" She twisted in his grasp, raked his cheek again, sobbing.

"Please!" he begged. "Your father —"

Treading on the shards of mirror, she had cut her bare feet. The white rug — the woolly pelt of some animal — was spattered with red. "I hate you! Damn you, I will *not* be treated so!" Wildly she tried to kick him, her tresses in disarray. "Something warned me — I should have known —"

Goaded into anger, he slapped her across the mouth. "God damn it, stop acting like a spoiled child!"

Wide-eyed, she stared, a hand fumbling where his blow had smeared the paint.

"Do you think I'm some sort of whore, to trade my — yes, damn it, my love for money? You're beautiful, and it's all I can do to resist you, Flora Lamon! But I did, and I'm glad I did! You *need* someone to refuse you from time to time! This was the time!"

"You — you *struck* me!"

The heavy brass handle of the door, an artifact in the form of the rearing lion, clicked to and fro. "*Señorita?*" It was the voice of Luz, the maid. "Are you all right, mees?"

Without moving her eyes from Jay, Flora spoke. Her fingers continued to caress the bruised mouth. "Go away! I'm all right!"

"Your papa want to know —"

"Go away, damn it!"

"*Sí, señorita!*"

Flora continued to face him, breast heaving, her eyes uncertain.

"Yes," he went on, picking up the overturned lamp, "I struck you! I never hit a woman before that I remember, but sometimes it's the best way." Gathering her in his arms, he carried her to the bed, laid her on the brocade coverlet, "Your foot is bleeding."

Her eyes followed him as he picked up his black valise, took out alcohol and a roll of bandage along with a small pair of scissors. "Perhaps I demeaned you. I didn't intend to. But you demeaned me also! I am not to be bought and sold!"

He pulled a splinter of glass from the flesh of her foot. She did not flinch, only stared at him with pent-up fury.

"I'm trying not to hurt you."

Her breasts rose and fell under the pattern of birds, flowers, and pagodas. "That does not hurt as the — the *other* did!"

He bandaged the cuts and closed his valise. "I have a little money of my own put aside," he lied. "A bequest from my mother. Somehow I'm going to keep the hospital open; it's badly needed." At the door he paused. "I hope the cuts don't become infected. I'll call

153

on you again and see how you are coming along." He bowed. "Ma'am — good day."

Not looking at her directly, he was still aware she was watching him. Risen on her elbows, the hair a tumbled mass and her face pale — almost waxen — with that same basilisk stare she watched him go. It frightened Jay more than when she had cursed and scratched him.

Spring blended almost imperceptibly into early summer. Thin patches of green from winter rains bleached out; around Mohave City the hills became the sterile gray Jay Carmody remembered from almost a year ago. The mill ground on, stacks belching acrid smoke. Andrew Lamon lay fuming and fretting in his bed above the town, issuing endless and confusing orders. Wagstaff's hired ruffians stalked the town, alert for evidence of rebellion among the surly miners. Jay Carmody became increasingly worn and haggard trying to deal with the flood of patients. Word of the new doctor traveled as far as Halfway Bend, Granite Point, Hawk Springs, and Tyson's Well. Sick and injured people came to him walking, riding, or carried in wagons or litters.

"I'm worn out," he said to Sarah Iredale one night, moodily eating the lentil soup she had made. "I'm plumb worn out!"

He was physically weary, but inside he also felt dispirited and uneasy. The encounter with Flora Lamon in her bedroom had left him apprehensive and gloomy. Sarah, too, had noticed. "You're so different the last few days," she said. "Is there — is there something you want to talk about? I'm a woman, you know. Women are good at things like that." Gently she touched his hair. "I declare — you're getting gray! There's a place here —"

Quickly he reached up and took her hand. Dr. Musgrave's Parisian Tonic! In his preoccupation he had forgotten the regular applications necessary to keep Dr. James Carmody's hair a dark brown instead of Jay Carmody's naturally straw-colored locks.

"I — I always had a little gray," he said. "Even when I was young. Very young. It runs in the family."

She persisted, looking at his hair again. "It's long, too. I must cut it again."

He ate the last of the soup. "When I have time, Sarah."

"You really must not work so hard. You'll kill yourself."

He shook his head. "The Carmodys are tough stock."

Carefully she put the plate and spoon back in the napkin-covered basket, taking a great deal of time. "I ought to hurry back. Papa's alone, and he's become so irrational lately! And I've got tomorrow's lesson to prepare for the scholars."

"You, too, Sarah — you mustn't work so hard. The school, and the major, and helping out here —" In a quick rush of feeling, he took her hand, pressed it hard.

"I — I will stay tonight if there is anything I can do! The Iredales are tough stock too, and I take very little sleep!"

In the back room Jay had several patients: a case of dropsy, old Don Jaime with a bad heart, a miner whose hand had been mangled in a hangfire blast at the Big Bug mine.

"No," he said, "it's not necessary. Concepción and María are here, and they will stay the night." Gnawing at his knuckles, he stared into the rays of the lamp. "It's medical supplies we need, and food, and blankets — they all take money!"

Still she lingered. "How is Mr. Lamon?"

He laughed, a short hard laugh. "I would be the last person to know! He won't let me near him!"

"Perhaps Miss Flora will come in to tell you."

"I haven't seen her lately either, I'm afraid."

Carefully Sarah adjusted the folds of the napkin covering the basket. "I have taken three of the most promising Mexican children into my school. Deputy Wagstaff came today and said Mr. Lamon was very angry when he heard about it. Mr. Wagstaff said I was to tell the children not to come again." Her chin lifted. "I told the deputy the school was *my* business, and that peace officers had no business there unless they were pursuing criminals, which he was very unlikely to find!"

Jay closed his eyes and sighed; after the hot soup he was sleepy. "Good for you!"

It was a hot night, yet Sarah went to the door and closed it, pulled the curtains. Curious, he watched her.

"I — I've got something to tell you." She sat near, basket poised on knees. "I hardly know how to go about it!"

"Whatever is troubling you, Sarah, you can always tell me."

"You — you remember the night that boy stole the nugget at the Vulture Mine, and came here so dreadfully wounded?"

"Roberto Díaz. Old Pedro's grandson."

"Yes. Well — they searched the hills and never did find the nugget they claim he stole. But I know where it is!" Fumbling in the wicker basket, she took out something heavy wrapped in the Yuma *Sentinel*. Holding it in both hands, she laid it on the desk before him. Unfolding the paper, she revealed a fist-size nugget gleaming in the mellow beam of the lamp. "He — Roberto Díaz — had it in his hands when he staggered in here. He gave it to me, almost with his dying words, and asked me" — her lip trembled in remembrance — "he said it was for *la gente* — his people — and asked me to keep it for them."

"Good Lord! That thing" — Jay hefted it in his hand — "it weighs five or six pounds!" Carefully he examined it. "Looks almost pure!" Taking his scalpel, he probed; the metal was soft. A shaving peeled off to lie shining on the desk. "It must be worth over a thousand dollars!"

Sarah took a small shuddering breath. "I've been scared to death with it under my bed! That night — maybe you remember — I tried to tell you Roberto had given it to me. But you and Deputy Wagstaff were arguing outside the door, and you didn't hear me. Then I decided you had enough troubles, and I didn't want to bother you. Still and all, I didn't want to give the nugget back to *them*, so I kept it."

He was staring hard at the nugget, envisioning all it represented, and did not at first hear the clanging bell.

"Listen!" Sarah said. "What's that?"

Jay went to the window and opened it. "Trouble at the General Kautz!" Calling to the boy Luis to bring the mare and trap around, he rolled the nugget up into the *Sentinel*, looking around for a place to put it.

"You did right, Sarah! I'm proud of you! We'll use it for *la gente*! Really, it belongs to them anyway! Good Lord, where can I hide it?" Casting about the room, a loose board squeaked under his boot. Snatching the poker from beside the stove, he pried the board up and dropped the nugget into the hole, stamping the board down with his heel.

"Can I go with you to the General Kautz? Maybe I can help!"

He looked at her a long time, listening for the sound of his trap in the street outside. "No. You've done enough for one woman, believe me!" Taking her face in his hands, he kissed her on the lips. "Sarah," he muttered, "I love you!" Embarrassed, he turned and ran blindly for the trap. He forgot his valise, and blundered into his office again. Sarah held it out to him.

"You'll need this," she said softly.

"I — I guess so," he said, and blundered his way back out. "Hurry!" he ordered Luis. "God damn it,

158

hurry!" It was almost as if he were anxious to flee from Sarah Iredale and the folly he had just committed.

At the General Kautz, a half mile east from the Vulture, all was confusion. Dineen was there, cursing, while Wagstaff and Singer confronted a muttering band of miners. Rubén Macías, miner's candle still flickering on his cap, shouted at the superintendent.

"I tell you many times — *las vigas*, the timbers, are rotten! They squeak, they talk, they sing — always they tell us, *por Dios*, that something soon fall down! Now look what happen!"

"What's this all about?" Jay asked.

Dineen, sweating in his white suit, was angry. "Timbers gave way in the Rat Heaven Drift! God damn it, we've been taking over two thousand ounces a month out of there! Now what in hell are we going to do?"

Jay hurried toward the gallows frame where the cage had come up, disgorging excited miners. "I'm going down there and see if I can help! Are you coming?"

Dineen looked uncertainly at Wagstaff and Singer. "You sure you can handle them?"

Holding the shotgun ready, the deputy said, "I'll take care of it!" Poking the muzzle of the weapon into Rubén Macías' belly, he drove him back. "In the name of the law, disperse! This is an illegal assembly!"

The Rat Heaven Drift was deep, with millions of tons of overburden. At the bottom of the shaft the scene resembled a woodcut from Dante's *Inferno*. Jay stumbled through clouds of dust lit by flaring torches, slipping in gumbo, falling and cutting his hands on piles of the worthless quartz called "gangue." "Down this crosscut!" Dineen pointed. His white suit was already smeared with mud.

From the vapors a dirty face swam into Jay's vision. A miner said, "*Por acá, señor doctor!*" and took his elbow. Dineen followed, stumbling, falling, cursing.

"Are there injured?" Jay asked. "*Hay heridos, amigo?*"

The guide shook his head. "All" — he slapped work-hardened palms together — "all smash, I think!"

When they reached the mouth of the Rat Heaven Drift, they found a massive fall of stone mingled with splintered timbers blocking the passage. In the light of torches men labored, staggering and grunting as they rolled away rocks, pried at boulders, tugged at great wooden baulks.

"Rigoberto!" one man called. He looked wildly around. "Does anyone hear him?"

"Rigoberto his brother," Jay's guide muttered. "*Su hermano!*"

Tugging at an iron bar, a miner worked loose a key boulder and rocks rolled down. The workers scattered; one man limped away on a mashed foot, but returned to dig again. Savagely the *mineros* toiled, cursing and praying at the same time.

"*Las vigas!*" a sweat-dripping giant shouted to Dineen, pointing. "*Ay, cabrón!*"

Dineen stepped sidewise quickly to avoid a bushel-basket-size boulder rolling down the slope. "What did he say?"

160

No Spanish! Jay thought. *He has been bossing these people and he hasn't troubled himself even to learn a smattering of the language!* He didn't answer. Instead, he dropped his valise and began to help in clearing the collapsed tunnel. Dineen grabbed his shoulder to shout in his ear. "Don't bother! The drift is probably choked for a hundred yards or more!"

"You don't know!" Jay protested. "How can we be sure some of those poor bastards aren't in there waiting to be dug out?"

"Because the whole thing was going to go soon! We were waiting for a shipment of post-and-cap from San Francisco. Come on — there's nothing to be done here!"

Tugging at a slab of rock, Jay straightened, "You mean you let them work in Rat Heaven Drift, knowing that — that —"

"Mining costs lives," Dineen said curtly. "It always did, always will."

Cabrón! Jay thought savagely. *Ay, cabrón,* indeed! The term was a deadly insult, but it fitted Dineen and the whole Lamon gang! Doggedly he went back to rolling away rocks, helping pull out broken timbers. One of old Pedro Díaz's many grandsons worked beside him, saying, "*Muchísimas gracias, señor doctor!* You are a good man, you are one of us. *Ay, Cristo* — so many rocks!"

The portion of the Rat Heaven Drift leading to the main tunnel became almost choked with the debris they had cleared; they labored between two rocky piles.

Someone went to ask that the burro-drawn ore carts take away the debris, but was refused.

"What did they say?" Jay asked, chest heaving and clothing soaked with sweat. He had lost the sole of one of his boots. Blood dripped into his eye from a cut on his forehead where he had run into an overhanging ledge.

The messenger spread his hands. "They say no! No use, *no sirve para nada!*"

Jay's anger exploded. "By God!" he said, *"I'll* talk to them!" He turned, intending to clamber over the debris and take the cage to the top. He would not let them condemn other men to death. But Deputy Wagstaff stood behind him, still casually holding the shotgun in the crook of his arm.

"Come on, Doctor! You don't belong down here!"

Jay wiped his chin with the back of his hand. The hand came away smeared brown with Dr. Musgrave's Parisian Tonic. Quickly he rubbed it on the seat of his trousers. "Look, can't you get them to haul away this stuff? Men may be trapped!"

Wagstaff pulled him away. "Dineen says to get you out of here. You're just encouraging them!"

"Encouraging them?"

"Anyway, it doesn't look good — a white man working side by side with greasers! Come on!"

"Who the hell is Dineen to tell me what to do? I was hired by Andrew Lamon!"

Wagstaff smiled his grave smile. "The old man is sick in bed. Miss Flora is running things now. She's heard all about the rockfall, and it's her instructions —

everybody out of the drift!" Some of the newly hired deputies crawled toward them over the high-piled rocks, and Wagstaff told the workers, "All right, now — everybody out! There's no use doing anything more. It's hard lines, but the men in there are dead — or soon will be!"

The sweating giant looked at Jay, then at Wagstaff. "No," he said. "We work! We keep working!" Pedro Díaz's grandson fingered his sleeve, where a hidden knife must be strapped to his forearm. "We work," he insisted. "We —"

In the narrow confines the roar of the shotgun was shattering. Wagstaff seemed hardly to have moved, but a rain of pebbles and rock dropped from the roof of the tunnel. "I don't want to hurt anyone," the deputy said. "Move, now — all of you! There are other drifts to work in, and you're wasting Mr. Lamon's time and money!"

"That's right!" the man called Singer growled. He prodded the giant with a carbine and the big man knocked it spinning from his hand. Pedro Díaz's grandson edged closer to Wagstaff, right hand tugging at his sleeve. Wagstaff saw, and lifted the barrel of the shotgun. Quickly Jay pushed the young man aside, murmuring "*Cuidado, joven!*"

Wagstaff smiled. "Doc, maybe you're one of the ringleaders we've been looking for. Speak the lingo well enough, don't you?"

"*Es imposible pelear contra fusiles,*" Jay muttered. "We can't fight against guns. There will only be more deaths."

Slowly the men dropped pry bars, shovels, picks. "Rigoberto!" someone called. "*Yo no olvidaré! I will not forget!*"

With the deputies on each side, weapons drawn, the exhausted company, Jay at their head, climbed the pile of debris and shambled toward the cage that would take them into the world of a June afternoon. When they got there, they found that Rubén Macías was in jail on charges of inciting to riot.

Seven men had died in the Rat Heaven Drift. Widows keened, families wept. Daily, black-clad women accompanied by solemn children visited the grave sites on the windswept hill and left bunches of spring wild flowers — sore-eye poppies, sun-drops, and four-o'clocks — in broken cups and tin cans filled with water. Quietly Mex Town seethed and bubbled, but it was not yet *la hora* — the time.

Hagop Aroutunian one day died peacefully in his bed above the Climax Store. His widow left for Sacramento to live with a niece. Flora Lamon hired a new storekeeper, a Chinese named Ah Sing. Her father, hitching slowly about the house with the aid of a cane and help from the small nephew of Amalia, the cook, disapproved Flora's action, declaring himself now recovered. There were rumors that the two quarreled bitterly.

Jay felt sorry for the red-eyed Mrs. Aroutunian. Still, as a formality, he crossed off Hagop's name in his small black book. Looking at the other names, however, he began to feel uncertain. Billy Dysart had proved too easy a target, unworthy of Jay's passion. Monk Griffin's defense of the drunken Mexican miners made Jay wonder a little. Had he misjudged Monk? Too, Homer Fox, the blacksmith, made new hinges for the sagging door of Jay's office. Luke Hodge, at the livery stable, was really a nonentity. Besides, he had probably been coerced into voting for the hanging. George Crisp, the man in the nautical cap at Jay's "trial," was fired one day for drunkenness, and had disappeared.

At first Jay had been content with the idea of the selective ruination of the instruments of his humiliation. Now, it seemed, they had only been the messengers; the bad news was the Lamons, father and daughter. Confused, uncertain, he took out his mouth organ and blew gently into it; it helped him think. But while he was making mournful music, Polonius Yount came unexpectedly into the office, bearing a bowl of stew his wife had prepared. Quickly Jay put away the mouth organ. Even foolish old Polonius might remember a night in the Mohave City jail, with a condemned prisoner softly playing "Dreaming Sad and Lonely."

"How are things with you, Polonius?" Jay asked.

"I got no complaints."

"How are you getting along with Wagstaff?"

Polonius licked dry lips, stared into space. Finally he said, "He's a Goddamned brute, that man."

"I know."

"Don't tell no one I said so, will you? My advice is to — to —" He broke off, staring again. He was not the cheerful and sprightly Polonius Jay had first known.

"He's got an evil temper, that Wagstaff. Him and Emmett Dineen has nigh come to blows."

"About what?"

"Macías. Rubén Macías. Dineen claims Rubén's too good a worker to lose. Wagstaff says he's going to take Rubén to Prescott for trial. Even the Lamons — the old 'un and the young 'un — can't decide what to do."

"Then there's no immediate danger to Rubén?"

"Not till they decide, I guess."

The *Cocopah*'s whistle sounded, a deep melancholy blast. The stern-wheeler was steaming downriver, and would tie up for the night to unload cargo for Mohave City. Jay made a decision; he would have to move fast.

That night he went to Mex Town. In response to his message via Luis, old María's grandson, the *casa* of Jorge Macías was filled with intent-faced *mineros*. Eagerly they listened to Jay's words, delivered in the mellifluous Spanish he was now beginning to master — and enjoy.

"No people," Jay said, standing before them in the flickering light of a candle in a wall sconce, "should have to suffer so. When *la gente* are treated as *esclavos* — slaves — it is only right they should fight for their freedom."

Jorge Macías shrugged. "Rubén is in the jail. We have no leader."

Jay felt power; a proper revenge was at hand. "Guns. You wished you had guns, *señores*."

The giant from the General Kautz spat into the dust of the floor. The man whom Jay remembered calling "Rigoberto!" — the man who had lost his brother in

166

the rockslide — muttered, "Where can guns be gotten? We have hardly enough money to buy food for our children! We can not even pay our good doctor when he cures our sicknesses, makes our children well, brings out our babies into the daylight!"

"I will get you guns," Jay promised. He did not speak of the nugget; there was no time for extended discussion. He turned to Paco. "*Joven*, I heard you speak of a Señor Agustín Obledo de Macías, your relative, in Yuma. He has a store there. He sells guns, you say."

"*Verdad, pero —*"

"Jorge Macías, *amigo* — I want you to write me a note to Don Agustín. I will tell you what to say."

Jorge spread his hands. "I do not know how to write!"

"Then I will write it in my bad Spanish, and you can make your mark."

There was a chorus of questions; Jay raised his hand. "*No hay tiempo, amigos!* There is no time! Trust me, that is all I ask."

The same night he visited the Lamon mansion. Seeing Deputy Wagstaff's buckskin tied at the hitching post, he nodded grimly. Amalia answered the door, and seemed uncertain when Jay asked to see Andrew Lamon. "He is in bed, *señor*, and I not know —"

"Miss Flora, then."

Amalia looked doubtful, but said, "Wait here, *señor*. I find out."

He did not particularly want to see either of them, but it was necessary for the secrecy of his plan. Finally

Flora herself came to the door. She looked pale and drawn; her hair was in disarray, and her feet were bare. "Well?"

He bowed, formally. "Ma'am, I wanted to tell you that I will be gone from town. As you know, I have been running low on medical supplies. There is a large warehouse in Yuma, Coates and Stockwell, which regularly receives supplies from San Diego by freight wagon. I intend to go down on the *Cocopah* and look through their stock. Depending on Captain Thorne's schedule, I should be back within a few days."

"As you wish."

"Is your father well?"

"You know his condition."

"Yes." He nodded, bowed again. "Good night, ma'am."

Halfway down the steps, she called to him. "Jay?" In the doorway the lamp in the hall outlined her figure. It seemed somehow pathetic, childlike; the sight made him uncomfortable. Still — she was the enemy.

"Yes?"

The ripe-wheat hair, backlighted by the rays of the lamp, swirled about her shoulders; her face was in darkness. "Nothing, really. Yet — I did not mean to seem brusque. Father is very ill and won't hear of medicine. I think most of it is due to the troubles at the mines. The company has such heavy commitments to eastern bankers for our new diggings in Peru. But — thank you for asking."

"Good night, Flora," he said, and departed.

Captain Thorne gave him free passage. "For all you've done for that benighted town," Thorne observed, spinning the big oaken wheel as the *Cocopah* splashed downriver, "you can ride free on my vessel anytime, Doc!" After the shallows below Mohave City, he turned the wheel over to the mate and sat beside Jay on the hurricane deck, watching *Cocopah*'s wake. "Damn me — I don't know how a feller decent as you manages to get along with those Lamon folks!"

Jay smiled. "I've found a way," he said, feeling the nugget weigh heavy in his pocket.

CHAPTER
TEN

He returned to a Mohave City that moiled in fear and confusion. Deputy Wagstaff had been killed in his office, a Mexican knife deep in his back. Paco and his father, Jorge, were in the jail, along with Rubén Macías, all charged with conspiring to kill Wagstaff.

"Mr. Dineen found him!" Sarah shuddered. "He was lying in a pool of blood. He'd only been dead for a little while, they say."

"But — Paco? The boy can hardly walk!"

"They say he and Mr. Wagstaff had words a few weeks ago."

"But why Paco's father — Jorge?"

She was bathing the forehead of an injured miner and before she spoke dipped the cloth into a pan of water. "They say the Mexicans planned it as a conspiracy."

"Who, pray, are 'they'?"

"Mr. Dineen, and the Lamons." She moved to the bed of an old Papago woman with a face seamed and crazed by time. "They say they're going to make an example of the Macías."

He rubbed his unkempt beard. It was a Saturday morning, and very hot. "If Wagstaff is dead, who's running things?"

"That man named Singer — you know. He and his bullies have taken over, and they're brutalizing the poor Mexicans. Their women are afraid to come into town anymore, and the men hide out at night and no one knows what they're doing." Her voice was tense. "There's going to be trouble!"

He took her in his arms, kissed the white line of the part in her hair. She did not know that it comforted him more than it comforted her. For a while she wept. Then she pressed hands against his chest and looked up with tear-wet eyes. "Excuse me! I — I didn't mean to break down like that! It's been very hard, trying to run the place with you gone, and the school, with all the trouble and everything. My scholars are frightened and aren't learning the way they should. The three Mexican children I had — their mothers won't let them come anymore, so Mr. Lamon has had his way."

As he always has, Jay thought.

"But weren't you going to bring back some medicines and things?"

For a moment he was caught off guard. "Well, you see, they were very heavy, and it took time to pack them. They'll probably be on the next boat. The *Cocopah*'s already gone up to Hardyville, but they'll probably be shipped on the *Explorer* or the *Nina Tilden* or one of the others."

He sat down at the desk, gnawing at his knuckles again. "How's your father?"

"With all the confusion in town, he thinks it's Sheridan's men raiding! I had to hide the big old pistol he carried in the war."

171

Mrs. Hodge came in, complaining of the catarrh, and Jay gave her a few of the sugar pills she declared stopped the attacks. Putting a fifty-cent piece in his hand, Mrs. Hodge peered out the window, clutching the old black umbrella that served as a parasol against the heat of early summer. "I declare — a lady can't hardly walk down the street without being accosted by those ruffians! It's a shame! I can't wait till the county gives us a proper deputy and sends those vagabonds packing!"

Deputy Wagstaff was buried in the desolate cemetery above the town. Most of the whites attended. Emmett Dineen and Flora Lamon were there, riding in the Whitechapel surrey with Andrew Lamon, shrunken and motionless, facing them. Since Jay had been in Mohave City he did not remember Lamon ever leaving his mansion, instead only watching the scene below through his brass telescope, like a spider central in its web. During the services, read by Dineen for lack of a preacher, the *patrón* remained in the surrey, big hands folded over a cane. Jay walked back to town with Monk Griffin, from the saloon.

"Output of the mines dropped since the troubles," Griffin said. "The Mexicans go down each shift, and they come up again in twelve hours like always, but they sure ain't digging much ore. No Fourth of July celebration this year, for sure, and I already ordered extra beer." At the swinging doors, he paused. "Come in for a cold one, Doc?"

Jay shook his head. "I don't drink much. Thanks, anyway."

172

Griffin pushed at the door, watched it swing to and fro. "Town's going to hell, sure enough! It ain't right, it never was right, to treat people so, even greasers! Guess I did my share of it, though, I kind of fell into a way of looking at things like the others did." He sighed, went into the dark cavern of the Empire.

For a moment Jay stood in the almost deserted street, sun hot on his shoulders through the black stuff of his shabby coat. One of the elbows had gone through, and Sarah promised to fix it. Below, the *Explorer* was unloading at the dock. He saw no sign of his boxes. What he did see, however, made the back of his neck prickle. Tuck? Tucker Stiles, come back to unmask him? It *was* Tuck — Jay knew the build, the pot belly, the meager chest!

"Tuck," he murmured. "God damn it — Tuck!"

His old companion had prospered; Jay noted the well-cut coat, the expensive valise, a glint of gold-rimmed spectacles. Tuck Stiles traveled without anything so cumbersome as morality. If Tuck thought there was money in it, he would betray anyone. Jay stood transfixed, feeling the heart thud against his ribs. Then the men toiled up the graveled road from the landing, puffing with effort. Jay saw that it was not Tuck, but a pleasant elderly man with a neatly trimmed pepper-and-salt beard.

"How do," he said to Jay, tipping his round-crowned felt hat and looking about.

"If you want a place to stay," Jay volunteered, "there's Mrs. Yount's, down the street. Sets a good table."

"Thank you, sir," the visitor said, and strolled on. Jay, shaken, wiped his forehead. He must get a grip on himself.

That night, well after midnight, he woke, hearing a strange sound. Someone in the hospital snored, broke off in a gurgle, and he heard Concepción's comforting voice. There it was — a persistent scratching. In bare feet and drawers he went to the window. He could see only a faint smudge of white in the blackness, but a small eager voice spoke. "*Señor doctor, soy yo — Luis!* You got guns yet?"

"No," Jay whispered. "But soon! *Qué pasa, muchacho?* What is it?"

Old María's grandson came closer, small hands gripping the sill. "I take you to a meeting of *la gente*. Can you come, *señor?*"

Quickly he slipped on pants, shirt, boots. Looking through the baize curtains, he was satisfied. Concepción slept in a chair, beside a guttering lamp. The old Papago woman was quiet. Carefully Jay stepped across the windowsill and into the night.

"Where, *muchacho?*"

"I show you, *señor.*"

Luis, trotting like a sure-footed goat, led him up the rocky incline behind Jay's office and along a ridge. Eyes unaccustomed to the night, Jay blundered behind him. Luis turned, a ghostly face with finger pressed to his lips. "*No haga ruido, señor!* We do not want to be heard!"

There was no moon, only faint starshine and the glowing wheel of the Milky Way. Far off a coyote

174

barked, then another. A chorus of yips sounded as the pack stalked an animal, probably a rabbit. Jay fell down, bruising a knee. His hand hurt where he had broken the fall, and a cactus spine stung his palm.

Luis hissed again. "I know!" Jay muttered.

Now they were above the town. Pausing to catch his breath, Jay looked back. On the high ridge he could hear a distant clamor. The night air smelled of acrid fumes and smoke; the windows of the mill glowed softly.

"Are you coming, *señor?*"

Jay turned and followed, forced into a trot as the small boy raced ahead.

Luis waved his hand to indicate a descent into a black defile, a canyon that dropped quickly down from the spine of the ridge. It seemed they were somewhere near the General Kautz, but Jay was not sure. Descending, his boots slipped. Again he went down, grinding hands into the shale in an effort to stop from falling — where? Into some bottomless abyss, perhaps; he could not see anything. But Luis hurried back to help him. "It is not far, *señor!* Come!"

Back of the ridge, the night was clean and pure. Jay smelled perfume of desert plants, felt cool as descending air rolled past him. Once he heard a dry thin rattle, and Luis pulled him aside. "*Cascabel, señor!* The rattlesnake! But he always tells us first, *verdad?*"

"*Verdad, Luis.*"

The boy guiding him, they clambered down a rocky defile and stopped before a gaping hole in the cliffside. "*Aquí, señor.* Here."

Wiping his brow, chest heaving, Jay stared at the blackness. "Where in God's name are we?"

"This is where the old September Drift broke through. They stopped mining here a long time ago, when the vein ran out. *Se acaba* — it is finished, now." Luis whistled a birdlike call. Two men, phantasmal in white *manta* pants and shirts, emerged from the mouth of the drift. "*Señor doctor?*"

"*Sí. Soy yo.*"

There was a flare as a match lit a candle, then a wavering light casting shadows on the rocks. "*Soy Lizárraga, Manuel Lizárraga.*" It was the giant Jay remembered from the day Rat Heaven Drift collapsed in the General Kautz. "Follow me, *señor doctor.*"

A bat flew by Jay's ear and he flinched. Following the candle, his boots splashed in mud and muck. He smelled dead things, decay. Down, down, down — the passage sloped endlessly. The air became warmer, damp, fetid. Still the candle bore on.

"Only a little farther, *señor*," Luis promised.

From a rocky alcove a man with a long machete called out harshly. Lizárraga stopped. "He is here," he said.

"*Pásele*," the man responded, stepping back into the crevice.

The passage widened, the low roof sloped upward. Jay heard muted voices. The darkness lightened and Manuel Lizárraga blew out the candle. "*Muy caro*, the candles!" he complained. "Cost a lot. That Chinaman worse than old Aroutunian!"

The voices grew louder. As they rounded a corner they saw the flare of torches. The *mineros* were there, many miners, falling silent as Jay entered the cavelike room. They took off hats, ceased talking. Many squatted in the rubble. One man sat on a rusting ore cart. Others perched on rocky ledges in cotton clothing, resembling white birds. "*Señor,*" they muttered, quietly and politely. "*Señor doctor.*"

Lizárraga spread his hands wide. "You see, *señor,* what we are reduced to! We must hold our meetings here, like rats, in the bowels of the earth. In the mines, in the mill, on the streets or in our own little town, we are prisoners, spied on and brutalized by those *rudos,* Señor Wagstaff's men. They have taken away our leader — our Rubén. In their jail they have also young Paco and Jorge Macías, held on false charges. Things have gone badly for us but still we hope! Meetings like this do nothing to free us, but we talk together, here, encourage each other, hope someday to be able to do more. We are simple men, with no learning, but even simple men must be free!"

There was chorus of approval. "*Verdad! Verdad! Eso es!*"

"You see," Lizárraga said proudly. "We have spirit, *señor,* if little else!" He motioned to a gigantic block of quartz gangue. "Now, perhaps, you will step up there, *señor,* and speak to us — tell us what you learned in Yuma from Don Agustín. Is there hope?"

Jay was not a public speaker. In grade school he had been shy and awkward when called on to recite. But he found himself almost eloquent when he stood on the

177

great chunk of gangue, looking down at the hopeful faces. Perhaps his ease was due to speaking in the fluid Spanish, in which he was now almost at home.

"I talked to Don Agustín. He will get us the guns and bullets, but it will take a few days. When they are ready he will pack them up and send them on the boat."

There was soft approval. One man cocked his finger, and muttered "*Pam!*" Others nodded with satisfaction.

"But there is one thing. First, you should send a delegation to Señor Lamon."

"*Una delegación? Porqué, señor?*"

"There has been enough trouble, enough killing. Now, I hear, there is not much ore coming out of the mines. Andrew Lamon needs all the gold he can get to pay his debts. If you were to send a delegation to talk to him —"

There was furious disapproval. "*No, señor!* We tried that! He will not talk to us! And that *puta*, his daughter, that Flora! No! *Por supuesto — no!*"

Lizárraga put a hand on his arm. "*Señor*, they drove us from the big house for being so insolent as to set foot on that beautiful green grass around the *casa!* They said we trampled the flowers!"

"Then I will talk to them!"

"You, *señor?* But the Lamons will not like that — their doctor speaking out for the miners!"

"That is a chance I will take."

A man in a ragged blanket jumped to his feet and raised an even more ragged sombrero. "Our *jefe!*" he cried. "We have a *jefe*, a leader!" Others took up the cry, "*Arriba el jefe! Viva el jefe! Viva el doctor!*"

178

Jay raised his hands in an effort to quell the tumult. "No!" he pleaded. "You don't understand! I — I can't be your leader! I'm just a — a —" He paused, uncertain. What *was* he? He had started to say, "I'm just a doctor." But that was not true either.

"*Viva! Viva! Viva!*"

Jay did not want to get further involved. It was one thing to feel sympathy for the miners, even to buy arms for them. But to abandon his own cautious plans, to come out openly, to stand as their leader, to face whatever perils might ensue, including arrest and prison, perhaps even worse, when the Prescott officials came to Mohave City, as they certainly would soon — His knees weakened as if they were filled with warm water instead of nourishing blood.

"They want you," Lizárraga urged. "They *need* you! You are their hope, *señor doctor*! There is no one else!"

Jay Carmody was a coward, he knew that. At the first sound of gunfire he would probably run like a rabbit, disgrace himself.

"*Viva!*" they were shouting. "*Viva nuestro jefe! Viva el señor doctor Carmothee!*" In Spanish, he remembered, an interior *d* became almost inaudible. "*Viva!*" Frustrated, Jay shook his head. Manuel Lizárraga raised a hand, trying to bring quiet. "They will hear you in the town, *amigos*! Those *bravos* will come after us!" The room was suddenly quiet, and he turned to Jay.

"All right," Jay said, unable to deny the acclamation, but inwardly damning himself for a fool. Still, if he *really* wanted to ruin the Lamons, father and daughter alike, he might as well go whole hog. What was it Tuck Stiles used to say? "In for a dime, in for a dollar!"

"But there is one condition," he insisted.

Lizárraga waited; the others waited, in silence.

"This must be a secret among all gathered here. A secret, until the time arrives!"

The big man raised an imaginary glass. "*Brinquemos*," he said. "We drink to that time! *A la hora!*"

For the first time in months the mill became totally silent. The sullen miners found many ways to slow down operations. An ore cart lost a wheel in a narrow passage. A giant-powder blast did little but make noise. In the mill, unknown contaminants made their way into the amalgamating pans and a batch of rich ore had to be reprocessed. But the silent protest was not without its price. There were beatings, maltreatment of Mexican women, and a shooting at the Big Bug mine.

"It sounds so funny," Flora murmured. "I mean — not hearing the mill. Listen how quiet it is!"

Together they sat in Andrew Lamon's upstairs office, shades drawn against the heat of the afternoon sun: Emmett Dineen in a wilted white suit, Flora, and Andrew Lamon huddled in the wheelchair. Even though the room was sweltering, there was a shawl about Lamon's shoulders.

"The sound of that mill was my life," he complained, reaching with a palsied hand for a glass of water. "It was the blood flowing in my veins!" In sudden anger he slammed the glass down; water spilled. "God damn them — after all I've done! If fair treatment and good pay won't do it, then I'll break them some other way — whatever it takes!"

Rising quickly, Flora went to him. "Father, you're not to get so excited! It's bad for your condition!"

"Condition? My condition!" Lamon's face was flushed; his fingers worked angrily at the ring with the rearing-lion crest. "I've got a brain, and I've got a will! I won't see what I've built fall down like a house of cards because of a bunch of ungrateful *peones*!"

"I'd give Singer free rein," Dineen advised. "He did good work over in Pinal County when the miners there were raising sand."

Flora, massaging her father's neck, was doubtful. "Mr. Singer has no finesse! And after all, he and his men don't have any legal status *I* know of. Mr. Wagstaff just hired them out of nowhere!"

"Legal status or not," Dineen remarked, fanning himself with a weeks-old *Sentinel*. "We've got to deal with this thing quick, and firm!"

A knock sounded at the door. Lamon croaked, "Who is it?"

Luz entered, made a curtsey. "*Señor, mees — el doctor está aquí.*"

"The doctor? Carmody?"

"*Sí, mees.*"

"That girl has been here for years and never learned proper English!" Lamon muttered. "Like all of them — lazy and ignorant!"

Dr. Carmody came into the room. Lamon thought he looked smaller than when he had last seen him. Dineen noticed the doctor's beard and hair were long and unkempt. Flora thought Jay looked haggard and unwell.

"Good afternoon." He looked about uncertainly, walking stick under his arm. "I wanted to talk to you, Mr. Lamon." In the face of their coolness he broke off, waited. Finally Lamon nodded toward a chair. Jay sat down, dusty bowler on his knee, conscious of the worn boots, one with the toe nearly out.

"I must say," Lamon grumbled, "that if we'd known a little more about what was going on in the mines, we wouldn't be in this pickle! You never gave me a single damned report!"

"Well, the fact is —" Throat dry, Jay coughed. "May I have a sip of water? It's awfully hot today."

Flora poured water, handed it to him. He did not look at her, yet was painfully aware of her presence.

"Ma'am, thank you. That's better, much better!" Again he cleared his throat, watching her walk back to the sofa, sit gracefully down with hands in her lap. "I — I — well, as you said, sir, I am much among the Mexicans, and know them well because of my professional work. The fact is they have asked me to come to you and plead for improvement in the mines: better working conditions, extensive retimbering, more pay —"

"What?" Andrew Lamon tried to rise from his chair. His face was incredulous. "You, sir, are you coming here as spokesman for those — those —"

"Father!" Flora spoke half in pleading, half almost as a command. "Calm yourself! You *know* it isn't good for you! And after all, Dr. Carmody isn't taking sides —

182

are you, Doctor? Anyway, we shouldn't punish the messenger because he brings bad news!"

"I am only here," Jay said stiffly, "to tell you what I know! What you do with that knowledge is none of my business!"

Dineen scowled. "We all know your feelings for those people!"

"I have feelings for all people," Jay said. "And I must tell you, sir" — he turned again to Andrew Lamon — "I must tell you that the *mineros* are ready for violence themselves. All — your pardon, ma'am — all hell is about to break out unless there is improvement!"

Lamon growled deep in his throat, good hand tightly gripping the upholstered arm of the wheelchair. But Flora spoke at once. "They are ready for violence? I am sorry for that, but what can they do? It seems to me Mr. Singer and his men are the only ones capable of real violence! Have your people" — she hesitated — "I mean, have the miners thought of that?"

"They have thought of that, but they are ready to die, if necessary, in what they consider a just cause."

Dineen started to speak, but Flora cut him off, her gray eyes hostile. "Dr. Carmody, violence serves no purpose! We all lose by it, eventually. As you must know, the Lamon mines are in financial peril. Father — we — greatly extended ourselves to finance the new mining developments in Peru. In the meantime, we are in debt to eastern banking houses. They are impatient for repayment of our loans. Rumors — even *rumors* of our failure to bring about order and restore production schedules would be quickly noised about back East!

183

The Mohave City mines might then be declared bankrupt, and we would all be ruined! The mines would close, and the Mexicans would starve! Do they know *that?*"

"It has been mentioned."

"And they still deliver us an ultimatum?" She was proud, now, and fierce.

"Call it what you will, ma'am — they are ready to meet violence with violence!"

"Then let it come! My father did not build the Lamon interests by being a milksop! And I am his daughter! Tell your friends to stop this foolishness and get back to work or they will be the sorrier!"

Lamon chuckled. "Bravo, Flora, my dear! I couldn't have said it better!"

Dineen slapped his knee with the folded *Sentinel*. "Threw down the gauntlet, didn't she, Carmody? By God, I like a woman that can send off sparks like that!"

Flora was not finished. "As for you, Dr. Carmody, I find your continued presence here intolerable!" The cheeks were flushed, and her breast heaved under the lacy bosom. One hand pushed back a lock of blond hair that fell over her brow. "As of the end of this month —" She paused, looking at a calendar. "This is the third of July. At the end of this month you may consider your services terminated. We will pay you a small bonus, because you have done good work here. Since you came to Mohave City there has been nothing but trouble. So I — we — bid you farewell."

Jay picked up his hat, brushed the nap with his sleeve, trying to keep his temper. "I will stay until the end of the month; I owe that much to my patients. But as for your bonus, you may —" Afraid of what he was about to say, he gritted his teeth. "Ma'am, good day. Gentlemen!" Slamming the door behind him, he stalked down the grand staircase into the blinding light. *Flawed!* he thought. *Flawed indeed, father and daughter alike!* Arrogance, pure arrogance, and a total disregard of whatever, whoever, might stand in their way! Nevertheless — he thought again of Flora in the boudoir, standing unclothed before him. *Beautiful — flawed.* A melancholy feeling swelled up in his chest.

For some time he had not seen Polonius. When he returned to the office the old man was sitting despondently on a packing case, looking into his ragged Union cap.

"*Nina Tilden* just come in. Understand she's got some freight for you."

Jay felt his heart beat faster. Things were fast approaching a climax — good or bad, he did not know. "Yes," he said carefully. "Medical supplies I bought at Coates and Stockwell in Yuma when I was down there."

Polonius licked his lips, shifted uncertainly. "Awful heavy. Big box."

"Mercury," Jay lied. "Used for sexual diseases."

Nervously the old man got to his feet. "Can we talk?"

"Of course."

Jay went to the door of his hospital where María and Concepción bent over a patient. Luis whittled in a corner. "*He regresado!*" he called. "I have come back." Quietly he closed the door.

"I can't keep it to myself no more," Polonius said gloomily. "Doc, I got to tell someone!"

Jay sat down at his littered desk. "What's on your mind, *amigo*?"

Polonius did not look at him. "I know who killed Wagstaff."

"What?"

"Folks sometimes thinks I'm an old fool, I know that! But I got eyes, and ears! And what I know makes me scared!"

Jay remained silent, waited.

"Doc, it was —" Polonius swallowed hard; his Adam's apple bobbed quickly up and down. "It was Mr. Dineen!"

"Dineen?"

"That's right! I was in back of the jail that night, fixing a bar in the window that rusted out. Mr. Wagstaff didn't know I was there, or forgot. Anyway, Mr. Dineen come in. He and Mr. Wagstaff got into an argument. Mr. Dineen wasn't satisfied with how the deputy was handling the trouble with the miners. Anyhow" — Polonius swallowed, consulted the interior of his cap — "anyhow, they got into an argument about Miss Flora. They was yelling something fierce! All of a sudden things quieted down. I heard someone kind of moaning and I sneaked back in and looked around." Polonius's voice quavered in remembrance. "There was Mr. Wagstaff laying on the floor, with one of the Mexican frogstabbers stuck in his back. I turned him over, and he give a gasp and — and passed away."

186

Jay got up, agitated. Wagstaff dead, Dineen delivered into his hands! "Judge" Dineen!

"You haven't told this to anyone?"

Polonius shook his head. "I ain't told no one except you, Doc! There wasn't no one I *could* tell! Who'd believe *me?*"

"Well, don't tell anyone!" Jay warned. "Let me think this over. Maybe there's something we can do with it." He laid a hand on the old man's shoulder. "This is true, every word?"

"I'd swear to it in court, with my hand on the Holy Scriptures!"

"You may have to!"

Polonius paled but remained firm. "Doc, a man can go just so long being kicked around and took for a idiot! I figure the time has come for me to stand up on my hind legs! I stick by my story!"

Jay found an envelope in a box, and a sheet of paper. "I'm going to write it all down, just as you told it. Then you can sign it, and I'll sign as your witness." Rapidly he wrote, finally handed the paper to Polonius. The old man read, moving his lips, and nodded. "That's her, all right." Jay handed him the pen, and Polonius carefully traced his signature. He handed the paper back to Jay, and spoke softly, very softly.

"Doc?"

"That ain't all I know."

"What do you mean?"

Polonius's lined face was a study in conflicting emotion.

"You're that feller they hanged last Fourth of July. You and the one called Tuck!"

CHAPTER
ELEVEN

In the heat of the office, shades drawn, the only sound was the ticking of the Regulator clock Mrs. Hagop Aroutunian had given Jay when she left town. Jay watched a fly climb the wall.

"Someone they hanged last Fourth of July? What do you mean?"

"Ain't no use denying it, Doc. I *know!*"

Slowly and deliberately, Jay reached for the flyswatter.

"What tipped me off first was that old song you play on your mouth harp. When I was younger I used to play the banjo. I remember that tune — something about 'weeping sad and lonesome.' You played it when you and that feller Tuck was in jail here, a year ago."

"That doesn't prove anything," Jay said. His mouth was dry; his heart beat off-rhythm. Trying to steady his hand, he picked up the flyswatter.

"That Parisian Tonic stuff you put on your hair, the stuff that comes off on your collar. Sometimes you was so busy your hair grew long and you didn't have time for Miss Sarah to cut it. It was long hair like the feller they hung, and blond in places. I closed my eyes and imagined a face that day they put the two of you on the

189

gallows — the beard gone, and hair a kind of blond color. Damned if Doc Carmody didn't come out looking like that feller they stoned out of town after they had their hanging pleasure with him!"

Jay swung the flyswatter and missed. The fly buzzed, caromed off the shade, bumbled away.

"Something else kind of funny, too," Polonius went on. "After Wagstaff was knifed, I found a letter on his desk. 'Twasn't right to read it, I guess, him being dead and all, but I was of a curious turn of mind. The letter was from the San Francisco College of Homo — Homo —"

"The San Francisco College of Homeopathic Medicine and Surgery."

Polonius nodded. "That was it! Anyway, seems Deputy Wagstaff had been curious, and was making inquiries. The letter said you wasn't never a student there and I burned it, so's it couldn't make no trouble for you. I got to admit I don't know the whole story, or what your game is, but I don't care. Maybe you was a doctor when you was hanged, which I misdoubt, or maybe you ain't one now — I dunno. But you're the best thing ever happened to Mohave City. So, whichever way your chip floats, it's all right with me!"

"You're right. I'm that man, Polonius, the one they hanged."

"What happened to the other?"

"Tuck? I don't know. After it — it happened, we broke up. I think he went East, to Baltimore or someplace."

"Listen," Polonius said. "Listen, Doc! If word gets out that Doc Carmody is the same man they had their fun with, I don't know how it would go. There's folks in this town that respects and admires you. There's others, like the Lamons, that don't take kindly to being made a fool of. So my advice to you would be to get out of town! I ain't told nobody, but could be there's others around that's noticed some of the things I noticed!" Painfully, the old man rose, blowing out his breath in a lingering wheeze. "Me, I got roots here. Guess I ought to stay, especial 'cause I know how Mr. Wagstaff got that Mexican knife in his giblets. If things gets too bad maybe I can use that someday to help folks. But you, Doc — you're free as a bird — free to get the hell out of here and go someplace where the air is better, say. That's my advice. Know what I mean?"

Jay nodded, put the envelope with Polonius's account of the murder into an inside pocket. "I know what you mean. But I'm committed too, old friend. I guess I'll stay on for a while."

Monk Griffin obliged Jay by bringing up on his wagon the heavy boxes from the *Nina Tilden*.

"Had to pick up the beer I ordered from Yuma anyway. Guess I'll have a fire sale on lager."

"I thank you for your help," Jay said.

It was evening. The sun was low but still stung; the air of early July was breathless and humid. For a moment Jay stood on the porch before his office. Then he saw the stranger again, the man in the well-cut coat and round-crowned felt hat. Uneasy, he went quickly in, closed the door. With Luis' help he dragged the boxes into his cubbyhole of an office.

"*Gracias, jóven,*" he said. "You must go home now. Everything here is very quiet."

He was unpacking the guns with a claw hammer when he became aware of someone watching. Turning, he saw Sarah, her eyes puzzled.

"Jay, what is this about? Why are there so many — so many guns?"

He was not an expert, but as a youth had done a great deal of hunting. His father often took him along for quail, ducks, and deer. Wiping grease from an old Sharps carbine with a heavily scarred butt, he saw with satisfaction that it was sound in other respects. The rifles — various makes, including older models of the Spencer, the Henry, and the Maynard — showed signs of heavy use. There were ten, along with a grab bag of pistols and revolvers — Remington, Starr, Colt.

"I can't tell you, Sarah," he muttered. "They have a purpose, though. You have to trust me till I can explain."

Curious, she came close. In her hands was a basin and a cloth. "I was bathing old Don Jaime with cool water when I heard you. Jay, what's going on?"

Laying down a bag of rimfire cartridges for the Henry rifles, he drew her to him. "Don't worry! It's nothing to concern you!"

"But I am worried! What are you doing with all those guns? You're a doctor — doctors make people well! They don't shoot them with guns!"

192

He kissed the lobe of her ear. "You must trust me, Sarah!"

"I *do* trust you, of course! You are about all I trust in an unhappy world!" She clung to him. "If anything happened to you, I — I —"

"Nothing will happen to me," he said, and was not so sure himself. "Believe me, what I do is for good. I know that, and you must believe it also." Gently he kissed her lips, touched the brown hair he had once believed colorless; now he saw within it glints of chestnut. "At present I have work to do."

She took a deep breath; for a moment it caught in her throat like a child after weeping.

"You must leave me now, Sarah. I am very busy."

She nodded, picked up the basin and cloth. Jay turned back to the task of inventorying the weapons and ammunition, saving for himself a Dragoon Colt with a good feel to it. The ancient revolver must be thirty years old, but it was well oiled and sound. Pulling the hammer back, he drew a bead on his image in the mirror. Then he let his arm sag. *Guns are to kill people with*. And he was supplying the guns. *My advice to you would be to get out of town. You're free to get the hell out of here and go someplace where the air is better.* Uncertain, he laid down the old Dragoon. It was full dark, except for a fringing of orange on the western hills. A faint breeze stirred the limp window shade. He *could* leave, right now, while there was still time. Things were getting out of hand. The *Nina Tilden* was alongside the wharf; he could easily escape the consequences of his meddling. Actually, he was a fool

193

to stay any longer in Mohave City. A leader? *Jefe* of the *mineros*? How would he act when put to the test, the *real* test?

Long after midnight he sat in the yellow glow of the Argand lamp. That too had belonged to the Aroutunians, along with the carpet in his office. With a pen he hesitantly scratched on a sheet of paper. How did one plan an uprising? It had seemed so simple — guns solved everything. But now the issue became complicated. Wait for another provocation, and then storm the mill with its rearing lion, as the Frenchmen did the Bastille? Take the jail from Singer and his bullies, and use it as a fortress? Jay was no military tactician; neither were the Mexicans. There was a danger in letting a lack of planning ruin the preparations. Nervous, he decided that the heat of the lamp was unbearable and turned it out.

Almost as if the winking off of the lamp were a signal, there was a rustle outside the window. The drawn shade was pushed aside; the craggy features of Manuel Lizárraga were framed in the starshine. "Señor?"

"*Sí,*" Jay whispered. "*Soy yo.*"

"You have the guns? We saw the boxes brought up."

"*Verdad.*"

Lizárraga whistled a birdlike call between his teeth. White-clad figures loomed ghostly out of the night.

"*Primero, una cosa!*" Jay warned. "One thing first, *amigo.* You are to take these guns and hide them. No one is to show a gun or fire a shot until I give the word!"

194

Lizárraga nodded.

"I am working on a plan of battle." Jay showed him the scribbled sheet of foolscap. "When the time comes we will hold a council of war, decide how to use the guns. But until then —"

There was a murmured answer of *"Adiós! Adiós! Hasta la hora!"* Then the white-clad figures were gone without a sound into the night. In Jay's teeming brain the whole thing suddenly seemed a dream, a disordered vision. Yet on the floor were the empty packing cases, on his desk lay the Dragoon Colt he had saved for himself.

At his desk he fell into troubled sleep. Near dawn, waking as first light crept through the window, he remembered where he was, what he had been doing. Discouraged, he picked up another sheet of paper. Meaningless scribbling! He did not yet have a plan — and the Mexicans were waiting on him, the *mineros* with their precious guns in leash. Shaking his head, he pillowed his cheek on his arms and drifted again into uneasy slumber, only to be awakened by the sound of gunfire. It seemed to come from the direction of Mex Town, along the river veiled now in mist.

"Señor?"

It was Luis, old María's grandson, peering across the windowsill.

"They say you come, quick! There has been shooting!" Luis held the tattered straw hat before him; his eyes were solemn with responsibility. "One of Señor Singer's men became drunk and had a fight with Jaime

195

Ribera. I know Jaime; he is a good boy and would never harm anyone. He —"

"Yes, yes!" Jay was impatient. "What happened?"

"*Pués, señor* — the man beat Jaime with the butt of his pistol and nearly killed him. Jaime's *papá* took one of the new guns and shot Singer's man in the shoulder."

Another rattle of gunfire sounded. A covey of birds rose squawking from the reeds along the river to soar into the sky, geese turning to gold as they flapped into the sun.

"Will you come, *señor?*"

Jay stuck the loaded Dragoon into the waistband of his trousers. "I will come," he said, dropping an extra loaded cylinder into his pocket.

In the street people milled about, alarmed. Luke Hodge, still in nightshirt, saw Jay first. "What's going on, Doctor? Do you know?" Monk Griffin, holding up his pants with one hand, held a bungstarter defensively in the other. Homer Fox, the blacksmith, grabbed at Jay's arm; his chin was stubbly, eyes thick with sleep. "Don't do no good to go down there! You'll get killed!"

Jay shook them off and hurried after Luis. The boy led him on a circuitous path through head-high greasewood and cat's-claw, emerging in damp sand at the river's edge below Mex Town. As they crept through the reeds, a shot whined through the river grasses. Shreds of green fell.

"Keep your head down, *muchacho!*" Jay called.

Splashing through the shallows, they came at last to the lower end of Mex Town. Faces of women and children looked out from crumbling adobes. Jay smelled the acrid tang of black powder mingled with odor of masa for breakfast tortillas. A bullet dug into a wall over his head, sprinkling him with crumbles and dust. "Down, Luis!" Jay warned. "Keep your head down, amiguito! Where is Manuel Lizárraga?"

They found him in an abandoned adobe behind an overturned trestle table of two-inch-thick planks. The thatched roof was smoldering. Through the window Jay saw one of Singer's men bob up from behind a rocky ledge in the canyon and loose a shot. The table quivered as the slug tore into it, but it did not penetrate.

Several mineros crouched around Lizárraga, fondling their new weapons but only watching, waiting.

"Lo siento mucho, señor," Lizárraga apologized. "We did not want this to happen, but Jaime's papá lost his head. I gave strict instructions but —"

Another of the Singer men rose from behind a bush and threw a flaming torch into the air; it thumped down on the thatched roof. Lizárraga raised his Starr pistol but the man had already taken cover.

"They are all out there," Lizárraga said. "Two of them went behind us, I think! Now they have us trapped between them and the river. It is not good."

A portion of the roof burned away and dropped onto the earthen floor; one of the defenders threw it out the window. "We can't stay here and be burned to death!" Jay said.

They fell respectfully silent. "What is your plan, señor?" a man finally asked.

Jay was confused, frustrated. Where, indeed, was his plan?

"Maybe," he suggested, "if I go out under a white flag, ask for a parley —"

Lizárraga shook his head. "I do not think so. These men want to kill us!"

"But they don't know we have so many guns, that we are ready to fight! After all, Jaime Ribera's *papá* only had one gun!"

Lizárraga started to take off his white *manta* shirt. "Felipe, hand me that bamboo stake in the corner. I will make a *bandera*, a flag, and —"

"No, *amigo*." Jay put a hand on the giant's arm. "I go."

"You, *señor*? But you are our leader, our *jefe*!"

Jay took the bamboo, tied his handkerchief to it. "All the more reason, I guess!"

Creeping around the overturned table and toward the door, he crouched low lest a shot through the window reach him. From the smoke-darkened shadows of the adobe he came suddenly into sunlight.

"Singer?" he called, waving the makeshift banner.

The flag toppled as a slug split the bamboo shaft. Something tugged at Jay's pants leg and his knee burned; dust exploded in spurts at his feet. Desperately he fled, dropping the flag and scuttling back into the adobe to shelter behind the heavy table. From the sunlit slopes triumphant voices jeered. "Lew, did you get him?" "Dunno, but he sure made a flat shirttail out of there!" "Wasn't it that doctor feller, the greaser lover?"

198

Jay pulled up his pants legs. There was a bloody crease across his kneecap. One of the slugs had struck a bootheel; his foot still tingled from the shock.

"You see, *señor*," Lizárraga said politely.

Jay was becoming angry. "There is nothing to do but attack!"

They looked from one to the other. "Attack, *señor*?"

He tore off the useless remnant of leather heel. "Attack is the only defense against those *cabrones*!"

More men crowded into the adobe, armed with knives and machetes. One patriarch carried a rusty scythe, another a gnarled club, a third had a leather sling and a handful of smooth pebbles from the riverbed. "*Señor*, what can we do?" In spite of protests, women crowded also into the adobe, anxious to stand beside their men.

Quickly, not knowing where the ideas came from, or even if they were sound, Jay gave orders. "Joselito, you and Pepe go out the back way and climb the hill behind them. Júlio, Roberto, and Nacho — I want you to go up the other side of the hill and hide yourselves. Try not to be seen!" Name by name — he knew them all — he disposed them, guessing about terrain, opportunities for cover, favorable angles for gunfire. "You," he instructed the men with knives, axes, scythes, and machetes, "stay behind, here in this place, until you are sent for. Maybe you will not be needed, but then again you might turn the battle if it goes against us." He put a hand on Lizárraga's sleeve. "Don Manuel and I stay here until you have all had time to take your positions. Then" — he tried to whistle, but failed dismally; his lips were numb and dry — "when the time comes, Don Manuel will whistle like a bird —"

"*Sí!*" Lizárraga grinned. Putting fingers to his mouth, he whistled the birdlike call.

"Then we will fire. Take any target you can find! Do not hesitate!" Suddenly he remembered. "Among us *gringos* there is a day we celebrate — our Day of Independence, *El Día de Independencia*, the fourth day of July. This is that day, *amigos*. May you gain freedom also this day!"

They crossed themselves. One by one, two by two, they moved out, carrying the precious burden of new guns, melting into the underbrush. Behind Jay and Lizárraga the rest knelt, crossed themselves, murmured softly to each other.

"Hey!" a voice called.

No one spoke. Mex Town was quiet in the morning sun, except for a rooster's eager crow.

"Hey, there!" Through the window Jay saw one of the Singer forces rise for a moment, look toward the adobe. Lizárraga raised his rifle but Jay pushed it down.

"Where the hell they gone? They was all in that 'dobe a minute ago."

Singer himself peered around a rocky shelf, revolver in hand. "Doc, you there? Anybody home?"

Five minutes, Jay thought. *Give la gente another five!*

Lizárraga was sweating too. Jay watched a bead of moisture slide down the thick brown neck, disappear under the shirt. The big man's finger twitched at the trigger. "It is hard to wait like this."

"I know, *hombre*."

More and more the gunmen exposed themselves, stepping cautiously from behind bushes, boulders, crawling over stony ridges.

"Singer!" Jay heard a new voice. He knew that voice; it was Emmett Dineen. "What the hell's going on here?"

"Bastards got guns somewhere! One of 'em jumped Jim Smike this morning. We chased him down here but he got away. The greasers was holed up in that old 'dobe, and they had guns. We seen 'em!" Singer rose from behind a clump of greasewood; taking off his hat, he scratched his head. "They *was* in that 'dobe! Something funny's going on. They're quiet as mice!"

"You ought to look out for a trap," Dineen advised. "They're sneaky, all of them. Maybe —" He broke off. "What was that? Something moved up there!"

Singer swiveled. "Where?"

Lizárraga moved close to the window, put fingers in his mouth. He looked to Jay.

"*Ahorita*," Jay said. "Now!"

The sweet birdlike sound wavered softly in morning sunlight.

"Now!" Jay said, springing to his feet. "*Amigos, vámonos!* Let's go!" The battle was joined.

Bursting out into the sunlight, waving the old Dragoon revolver, he yelled like a banshee, burning with the humiliation of a year ago. This was Jay Carmody's Independence Day, too; no more skulking, hiding, pretending; no more lying awake at night wondering if anyone was privy to his secret; no more Dr. Musgrave's Parisian Tonic!

201

"Yahoo!" he shouted. "Sooey, sooey, sooey!" It was how he used to call hogs on his father's bleak and unprofitable farm. "Yahoo!"

Orange flame exploded in his face and a ball creased the air near his ear. Almost blindly he pulled the trigger and saw one of Singer's bullies clutch at his leg, spin about, and stagger away, cursing. Manuel Lizárraga missed a shot at another man at close range. The two collided, falling in a fierce embrace. The giant's strength was too much, however. Lizárraga pinioned him with one hand, bashed him on the head with the butt of his pistol. "*Cochino!*" he spat. "Pig!"

From the rocky slopes above came a rattle of small-arms fire. The Mexicans were poor shots. Most had never been rich enough to own a gun. Those who had once possessed them were out of practice. But the sudden and unexpected onslaught panicked Singer and his crew, sending them reeling back through the canyon, down the dusty road toward town. The man Jay had shot limped after them, calling for someone to help him. Lizárraga raised his pistol and took aim but Jay knocked the weapon up.

"They're running away!" he said. "No need to kill without a reason!"

He snatched the sleeve of a Mexican boy who was scrambling down the hill with a rusty machete in his hand. It was little Luis. "Go back, *muchacho*, and tell the rest to follow us, but keep behind. The *cabrones* are running, but there is still danger!"

Waving his arm, Jay signaled the *mineros* to advance along the edges of the canyon to prevent a flanking

202

counterattack. He, Lizárraga, and several others took the road, weapons at the ready, watching for marksmen who might linger among the rocks.

Lizárraga was concerned. "I know where they have gone!"

"Where?"

"The jail. They have more guns there, more ammunition. They will lock themselves up, as in a fort!"

"Probably so," Jay admitted. How would he deal with that — a standoff? But there was no time to ponder. "*Adelante!*" he called. "Forward!"

In the town, everyone was inside. He saw Luke Hodge peering from the dusty window of the livery stable. The new Chinaman who ran the Climax Store stood in the doorway wringing his hands. "Why shooting? God damn!" Homer Fox, strange without his weekday leather apron, stood before the empty American Eagle Barbershop, Sunday Bible in one hand. "Doc, what's going on? Is it a revolution?"

"All of you get off the streets! Someone might get hurt!" As Jay spoke, shots rang out from the jail. Splinters flew from a post near his face. "Get off the streets! There's no quarrel with any of you! It's Singer and his gunmen we're after!"

The *bravos* were indeed barricaded in the jail. Jay heard a tinkle of glass as a rifle barrel was shoved through a window and the muzzle poked out. At the same moment he became aware of Sarah Iredale and her father. The old man was in a nightgown, carrying an unsheathed saber. Sarah tried to pull him back.

"Jay! Are you all right? What's going on? You're —
you're hurt? There's blood on your trousers, and your
face is bleeding, and —"

"I'm all right!" he comforted her. Taking Major
Iredale's arm, he drew him gently inside the
barbershop. "Sir, you're the reserves! Stay here, with
Sarah! We'll send a message when we need you."

The old man's watery blue eyes stared; the bushy
brows twitched. "Sheridan? Is it Sheridan's men?"

"Yes, but we've got them on the run!" Jay turned to
Sarah. "Don't worry, dear Sarah! Everything will come
out right, believe me! Stay here, out of sight, and take
care of your father."

Stiffly the old man saluted. "Yes, sir," he said. "Reserves!
A good general has always got proper reserves!"

"Hey, Doc!" someone called.

He sidled out the door, slid behind a corner of the
barbershop. It was Singer, calling from the jail across
the street. Jay signaled to Lizárraga. In response the
giant moved about among the crouching *mineros*,
ordering them here and there; some on the roofs to
cover the jail, others to circle around by the river and
guard the back.

"Hey, Doc!" The voice was insolent.

Carefully Jay edged around the worn boards, looked
across at the jail.

"You know we got them Macías boys in here with us?
In cells? All three of 'em?"

Jay felt a sudden lurch of his heart. In the heat of
battle he had forgotten. All three were still in the jail;
Jorge, Rubén, and the crippled Paco.

204

"Call off your greasers! If you don't, them three'll never get out of here alive! We'll cut their throats!"

"That's right!" someone behind yelled. "And don't think we won't do it, neither! Right, boys?"

There was a chorus of gruff agreement. "Sure will!" "Ain't slaughtered no greaser meat for a long time!" "We'll set fire to the jail and barbecue 'em, that's what we'll do!"

Lizárraga knelt beside Jay in the shelter of the projecting corner. "*Carramba!* They would do that, too!" He looked at Jay, face uncertain. "What to do, eh?"

A small breeze from the river sent up a curlicue of dust. It spiraled down the road, dancing and gyrating.

"What say?" Singer called.

Jay cupped hands to his mouth, called, "What do you want, then?"

"Can't hear you!"

"I said — what do you want?"

The wind rose, blew more steadily from the river. A cloud slid over the sun, and the wind turned chill. "Lay down your guns! Throw 'em all in a pile in front of the jail here!"

It began to rain, at first only a few drops pockmarking the dust of the street and tinkling on the corrugated iron roof of the barbershop. From rooftops, around corners, in dark doorways, Jay was aware of eyes watching him — dark eyes, Mexican eyes, *minero* eyes.

"Well?" Singer taunted. "Looks like we got you between a rock and hard place, don't it? What say, *señor doctor?*"

On another Fourth of July it had come down to this. The months of painful learning, the role-playing and deception, gradual acceptance by Mohave City and his realization that the people were not all evil — these milestones in his life were all past. Now Jay Carmody faced the real, the ultimate test.

CHAPTER
TWELVE

Not wanting to think anymore lest thought betray him, Jay started from the shelter of the barbershop. Manuel Lizárraga quickly pulled him back. "What you do, eh? *Carramba!*"

"I've got to go out and talk with them."

"No, *señor!* They shoot you down, and laugh!"

"Trust me," Jay insisted. "I know what I'm doing!" He didn't, really, but stepped into the street.

"Singer!"

There was no answer, only a rustling of the dust by a few drops of rain. The air smelled cold and hard. In the hush he finally made out Singer's bearded face at the window of the jail. The gunman raised his rifle, slowly and deliberately.

"I could blow your head off right now, Carmody or whatever your real name is, but I'm too much of a gentleman!" He laughed, waggishly. "What's on your mind?"

Jay removed the cylinder of the Dragoon, tossed it into the dust, moving slowly and carefully so he did not startle any nervous gun in the beleaguered jail. Then he threw the revolver itself down. "I'm unarmed, you can see." Slowly he walked toward the jail. The street was wide, wider than he had thought. Slowly he raised his hands above his head. Step by step he crossed the deserted street feeling sweat break out on his forehead. Heart pounding, knees weak, he knew again that shattering feeling on the gallows, but forced himself to move toward Singer and the broken window, the menacing snout of the rifle.

"Don't come no farther!" Singer's voice was tinged with alarm. "By God, I don't trust you! Stop right there!"

Jay stopped. "I've got a proposition for you!" The rain was heavier, now; it felt cool on his cheeks.

"You ain't in no position to make deals!"

"Hear me!" Jay urged. "Just hear me out!"

Eyes narrowed, Singer sighted again down the barrel of the rifle. Jay trembled. *Is this, now, the way I'm going to die? In a deserted street in the Arizona Territory, in the rain?* Forcing his voice, trying to keep it steady, he went on, choosing the words with care.

"There are armed Mexican miners all around the jail. Some have guns, others have knives and machetes. They're after freedom, and they'll do whatever is needed to get it. If anything stands in their way now, they'll swarm over it, and die if they must."

The hard eyes bored down the gun barrel. "I ain't much to palaver, Carmody. We got the top hand, and you know it. What about them three in the cells? Did you take into mind what can happen to them if you try any funny stuff?"

"They'll die, too, and be glad," Jay said, "if it will help to bring freedom to *la gente*. They know you'll kill them anyway."

Singer hesitated, finally spat through the bars. "I don't believe you. And you know what? I think I'll shoot you right now, right where you stand!" He pressed the stock against his cheek, squinted.

"Do that," Jay answered, "and they'll take the jail by storm and kill you all! Maybe not all." His lips were dry, and he licked them, feeling his heart pound slow and distant, like a muffled drum. *If they would die, I suppose I would, too.* "Not all! Maybe — ants, cactus needles first, a mouse under a tin pan on your belly while they build a fire on top. The mouse gets panicky and starts to dig —"

"Enough talkin'!" Singer snapped. He lowered the rifle, spoke to someone inside. Jay waited. Finally Singer turned. "What's the deal, then?"

"Just this — you and your people come out of the jail with your hands high and throw down your weapons. I guarantee we'll let you all go, then, wherever you want."

There was muffled colloquy inside — protests, wrangling, curses. After a while Singer returned to the window. "We took a vote."

Jay waited.

"We got your word we won't be harmed?"

"Yes."

Singer spat again into the street, rubbed a bristled chin. "I ain't got no use for you, Carmody. Anybody cozies up to greasers the way you do ain't a white man in my book. Still and all, I ain't never heard it said you went back on your word. So I guess we're bound to trust you. Looks like we got a busted flush, anyway."

For a long time there was silence in the jail. Then the door opened, and Singer walked out on the porch.

"Throw the rifle down," Jay ordered.

Sullenly the gunman complied. The rest filed out, sheepish and hangdog, and laid their weapons reluctantly on the pile. One ruffian hesitated, fist on pistol butt, staring about truculently. Manuel Lizárraga jabbed him with the muzzle of his Sharps rifle.

The man cursed, and dropped the pistol with a clatter.

Jay counted. "That all of you?"

Singer bit off a fresh chew of tobacco. He jerked his head toward the canyon where the fight had taken place. "Sim Brown's back there with half his head blowed off, and Kid Irby damn near cut in two with a machete. Snake" — he nodded toward a man with a bandaged head — "he got kind of creased."

"If you like," Jay offered, "I'll take a look at the wound."

"The hell you will!" Snake growled. "You ain't no real doctor! Wagstaff said you wasn't, said it from the first, said he could prove it! You ain't gonna lay hands on *me!*"

Jay shrugged. To Manuel Lizárraga he said, "Go *pronto* and unlock our friends." A group rushed into the jail, and moments later returned with Jorge Macías, Rubén, and Paco hobbling on his crutch. There was joyous reunion, with many *abrazos* — the hugs and squeezes between men that always made Jay uneasy. But it was only their way.

"*Amigo!*" Rubén Macías exclaimed, wringing Jay's hand. "So it is you who led the fight and got us out of that stinking jail! *Ay, gracias a Dios!* You are truly a *jefe*, a natural leader! I knew that when first I saw you!"

"These — these men did it," Jay stammered. "All these men did it! They were very brave."

Paco, too, embraced Jay. Jorge, the quiet one, simply beamed from ear to ear, all the while crossing himself.

Embarrassed, Jay fidgeted away from Paco's embrace. Jorge's big hand fell on his shoulder. "*Hombre*, I need something to fight with!" Joyfully he snatched up a rifle and shot into the air. Singer and his men shrank back, startled.

"You give us your word!" he protested.

"So I did." Jay pulled down the upraised barrel. "*Cuidado, hombre!* There is no more fighting to do — not with guns and machetes. Now it is a matter of talking to the Lamons, demanding our —" He broke off. *Demanding our rights*, he had been about to say. "Demanding your rights," he amended.

Looking sour, Singer kicked the dust. "Well, then — we got horses, at Hodge's place."

"Take them, then, and go fast. Don't ever come back."

"Can't promise that," Singer growled, but it sounded like bravado. "Come on," he said, and walked toward the livery stable, the rest following him, dispirited and impotent without their weapons.

Watching them go, the townspeople edged out into the street. "Good riddance!" Monk Griffin called after them. Homer Fox, Sunday-reading Bible still in a hamlike fist, said, "There was never no call for the Lamons to bring killers like that into Mohave City, no matter what!" Ah Sing, the Chinaman, was the only one regretting the departure of the gunmen. "Owe me three dollah, that Singer, for tobacco and two shirt!"

Running to Jay, Sarah Iredale threw her arms about him, her face wet with rain or tears. "That was the bravest thing you did, Jay! I'm so proud of you!" Old Major Iredale beamed and said, "Reminded me of a cavalry sergeant I knew! Took on a whole battery of artillery at Ball's Bluff!"

Jay found he had almost lost his voice, and coughed several times. "Dear girl, the Mexicans did most of it! I only helped out, you see."

Drawing back, still holding him by the arms, she looked strangely at him. The brown eyes, he decided, were really prettier than Flora Lamon's slate-gray; certainly deeper, and honest, very honest.

"What did that man mean — you're not a real doctor?"

He was grateful when Manuel Lizárraga touched his arm to interrupt the conversation. "*Señor*, we go now to talk with the Lamons?"

"Sarah," Jay said hurriedly, "I will explain later. Right now we must strike while the iron is very hot."

Hoisting him unwilling on their shoulders, the Mexicans bore him away. Singing, cheering, they carried him down River Street, past the mill, up the graveled road toward the Lamon mansion, sitting high and silent in its frame of rain-wet greenery. *"Arriba el señor médico! Arriba nuestro jefe! Arriba Don Diego!"* As they marched, the little band was augmented. Women and children from Mex Town joined them. The Mohave City townsfolk fell in, followed by a few Indians. By the time they stopped before the white columns of the Lamon mansion, they were two or three hundred. Jay, managing to slip down from the shoulders of his supporters, saw one of the heavy velour curtains upstairs draw quickly aside, as quickly draw back.

For a long moment he stood irresolute before the pillared mansion. Respectfully quiet, the people waited behind him. He blinked, feeling a sudden twinge of unreality. Excitement of the battle, elation after facing down Singer and rescuing the Macías — these faded before a wash of panic, blotting them out as sand castles crumble before the lazy wash of a wave.

"*Señor?*" Manuel Lizárraga asked.

The Lamons were rich and powerful people, with an international corporation that was traded on the New York Stock Exchange. *Sixty thousand ounces a month. New mines in Peru. Public officials bought and paid for.*

"*Señor*, you talk to them now, eh?"

Here were no shouts, no cheers, no heat of battle to excite. This was a different confrontation. Jay swallowed

213

hard, took a deep breath. *Flawed, all of them. Red-bearded Dineen, too.* But dangerously flawed, with the law behind them, law that Andrew Lamon had made his own. Uncertain, knowing only that something was expected of him, he turned. *La gente* stood there, patient and waiting. They looked back at him with gentleness, respect — trust.

"Yes," he said. "I — I will go up and talk with them now."

He mounted the first step. But Emmett Dineen, apparently waiting, threw open the big door. "What the hell do you want?" he asked. "And what is all this mob out here?"

Jay's shirt was torn, blood oozed down a pants leg from a grazing wound. He must look like a pirate with the Dragoon Colt stuck in his waistband.

"This is no mob, Dineen. This is a deputation of citizens who want to talk to Mr. Lamon. They have demands which must be discussed."

Dineen reddened. He stood wide-legged, blocking the doorway. "Demands? Who are you, or they, to make demands of anyone? A bunch of ruthless killers who assaulted our peace officers! I understand they killed two of Singer's deputies, and wounded others with smuggled firearms! Why, it's insurrection, and someone will hang for it!"

"We won't leave until we talk to Mr. Lamon," Jay said.

"Mr. Lamon is sick. If there's any talking to be done, you can talk with me."

Jay shook his head. "You don't run things hereabouts, Dineen. All you are is hired help. We want to talk to —"

Through the open door, brushing Dineen aside, came Flora Lamon. She was cool-looking in a summer frock, belted at the waist with a pink sash. The wheaten locks were done up on top of her head in a Grecian roll. Her arms were bare; the classic face pale, but composed.

"To me," she said. "You want to talk to me, I suppose, Dr. Carmody, since my father is ill."

Angrily Dineen snatched at her arm but she pulled it away.

"Flora!" he complained. "This is a man's job! You can't talk to them! Wait till Prescott sends help!"

"Emmett, don't interfere! I know what I am doing." She turned to Jay. "Will you come in, please?"

Slowly, pain in his injured knee, Jay limped up the steps, past the glowering superintendent, onto the broad veranda. He followed Flora into the hallway, up the stairway to the encircling balcony, across the lush carpeting toward the library. Dineen was behind him, and he could feel the heat of the superintendent's anger.

In the library-office Andrew Lamon sat huddled in the wheelchair, shawl about his shoulders. The room was muggy and stifling, windows closed and shades drawn.

"So it's you!" Lamon rasped.

"Yes, sir."

"Bad penny, eh? Damn, I was a fool ever to hire a doctor for those ingrates!"

Flora went to her father and adjusted the shawl. Dineen sweated heavily, his white coat stained, and held the Colombian hat tightly in red-furred fingers.

"I'm not a doctor," Jay admitted. "Not a real one, anyway." Saying so, a great burden seemed to fall from him. He went to the window, pulled the heavy draperies aside. Sun lit the gloom; the unseasonable rain had blown itself up the river.

"Not a doctor?" Lamon wheezed, heavy brows drawing together. Dineen's heavy face bore a sudden look of triumph. Flora stared, unbelieving. "Not — a doctor?"

"Today," Jay said, "is the Fourth of July — Independence Day. One year ago you all had your fun with two ragged unfortunates who drifted into Mohave City. I don't know whose idea it was, but someone thought a mock hanging would liven up the day, along with the free beer and band music and chuck-a-luck games."

Slowly Dineen shook his big head, grinning. Flora's eyes were wide in surprise. Andrew Lamon raised a shaky hand and pointed at Jay, making incredulous noises in his throat

"My friend Tucker Stiles and I were strangers. There's a long tradition of the stranger — the outsider, the man who might be evil, the man who could cause trouble. Mohave City was a little kingdom, you might say, and we were a danger to it!" Jay laughed, harshly. "Two scared and penniless vagrants! But that's the way

216

with kingdoms. They're built on fear. They can't stand the sight of anything that might challenge them, even unlikely challenges."

"That *was* you," Dineen blurted. "Now, Flora, I hope you admit I was right!"

Jay nodded. "Yes, that was me — and Tuck. Tuck went on to other things, but that hanging changed my life. I made up my mind I'd pay back the people who treated me so. What better disguise, then, than a doctor? People would never suspect a man of medicine. Fortunately, I'd had some medical training. I prepared myself further by a lot of hard work and studying. When you put that advertisement in the *Call*, Mr. Lamon, it was a stroke of good luck for me."

"I knew it!" In spite of his daughter's restraint, Andrew Lamon tried to rise from the wheelchair. "God damn you, Carmody or whatever your name is —"

"So I came back," Jay said implacably. "I came back with one thought in mind — to ruin you all. And by God — now I think I can do it!"

Escaping from Flora's arm, Andrew Lamon grasped his cane and staggered from the wheelchair, brandishing the heavy gold-headed stick like a weapon.

"Father!" Flora cried. "Emmett — help me!"

Lamon's mouth opened, gaping, like a fish needing air. "Rascal!" he howled. "You — you scoundrel!" He dropped the cane, both hands clawing the air. "You —"

It was Jay who caught him, lowered him gently to the rich pile of the carpeting. Lamon's once-powerful figure was rigid in his grasp, and a string of spittle ran from a corner of his mouth. The *patrón*'s eyes stared glassily upward.

"Father!" Flora knelt beside Jay, cradling the grizzled head in her arms. "Oh, help him!"

"He's killed your father," Dineen growled, standing over them.

Jay put an ear to Lamon's vested chest. "He's not dead."

Dineen pushed him roughly aside. "Then get away from him! Don't touch him! You're no doctor, anyway!"

"I'm the only man in town that knows anything about apoplexy, doctor or no doctor," Jay said. "Flora, get some of the help to carry him into the bedroom. You, Dineen, send down to my office and get my satchel."

"But —"

"Do as he says, Emmett," Flora said in a tight voice. "And quickly!"

With Andrew Lamon lying only in his drawers on a brocaded coverlet, Jay asked for a basin. "I'm going to draw some blood," he told Flora, stropping a kitchen knife on the edge of a stoneware basin. "Most medical authorities think this kind of thing results from too much pressure of the blood. I'll draw off a pint or so, and that should relieve some of the pressure."

Flora and Luz watched as he slit the vein, let blood flow in a puddle into the basin, then closed the wound with a tight bandage. "Can you hear me, sir?" Jay asked, looking down at the staring eyes.

There was only a twitching of the facial muscles, a faint mewling sound.

218

"Father!" Flora buried her face in her hands.

"I'm sorry," Jay said, wiping his hands.

Emmett Dineen came into the room with Jay's satchel. He threw it carelessly on the bed. "Flora, I told you all the time there was something funny going on! Wagstaff knew it too! Now you see —"

"Be quiet!" Furiously she turned on him. "I won't have another word out of you, Emmett!" To Jay she said, "What — what will happen now? I mean —"

He shrugged, took an almost empty bottle of Dr. Mintie's Vital Restorative from the satchel.

"I don't know. He may recover somewhat. Only time will tell." With the aid of Flora and Luz he managed to get a little of the Vital Restorative into Andrew Lamon's mouth, although the tightly clenched teeth made it difficult. "All that can be done now," he said, rolling down his sleeves, "is to keep him quiet, and hope for the best. I've done all I could do." With a sudden tingle of pride, he added, "Or maybe all a real doctor could do!"

There was a commotion below. Luz went out into the hallway, came back, fearful. "Mees, a big man down there, with *machete*. Want talk to *señor doctor*."

Jay went out, looked down. Manuel Lizárraga stood in the hallway among the potted palms, gleaming machete in one big fist

"I'm all right," Jay reassured him. "*Momentito* — wait!" He went back into the ornate bedroom. Flora sat on the edge of the bed, watching her father's labored breathing. Dineen hovered uncertainly at her side.

"I — I can't believe it," Flora murmured. "He — he was always so strong."

"I'm sorry," Jay said. "But it was bound to happen, you know. He is a very obstinate man. No doctor could help him if he refused treatment."

Chastened, Dineen asked, "Is there any hope? I mean — you're not a real doctor, but —"

When Flora looked at him, pain in her eyes, Jay tried to be kind, although he was not hopeful. "He may regain some of his senses, be able to sit up and be wheeled about. But there is a strong possibility he will not be able to speak intelligibly, and will remain confused."

For a moment he thought Flora was going to break completely. But she pulled herself together, blinked back tears, wiped her eyes with a fragment of lace. "I — I thank you for telling me the truth."

In sudden compassion, he said, "Damn it all, Flora — I never wanted this to happen! I know it's a great shock to you. Why don't you rest? I'll give you something to make you sleep. In the meantime, Luz and María and the rest can see to your father. The people outside can wait; we'll discuss matters later. In the meantime —"

"No." Her voice was firm. "There is a problem to be solved, and now I must solve it. Let us go into the library."

In the dimness of the book-lined room she sat in her father's chair behind the great carved desk. Dineen stood nearby, a possessive hand on the carved lion ornamenting the high back.

"So," Flora said. "A macabre kind of joke. You are that man, the man we hanged!"

"Yes."

"Returned to bring sickness and ruin."

He had a scathing reply poised on the tip of his tongue, but forbore. "As you wish, ma'am."

"I have never been one to run from a problem. My father taught me that, and I am his daughter. I will speak for him, Dr. Carmody. I do not want you to be under any misapprehension. You will find me as hard to deal with as Andrew Lamon." She looked down at her fingers, tapped them thoughtfully on the desk. "I might as well tell you — the mock hanging was my idea. I had seen a hanging, once, in Boston. The miners were restless, and my father and I thought it would be a good idea to put on a show for them. We thought it might be well to demonstrate that agitators would receive short shrift, as they say." She sighed. "Actually, I was bored with this dull place and the lack of interesting men! When I am bored, I am sometimes cruel and unthinking. But I never regret."

Jay remembered his last glimpse of the beautiful lady in the Whitechapel surrey that fateful day. Flora had been smiling. Feeling the Dragoon Colt pinching his lean waist, he pulled it out and laid it aside. "Your pardon, ma'am — I'm not all that used to guns." Remembering the smile, he added, "Perhaps I should say that during my time here I found the people of Mohave City weren't half bad. They were really just folks like me. The trouble was — they'd been infected with evil by the Lamons."

Dineen flushed, stepped imperiously forward. Flora waved him back.

"Go on."

"I discovered that you and your father, ma'am, were the real reason Mohave City was such an ugly and vicious place. So I found, through my medical practice, a weapon to save the town and regain my own self-respect."

"Very neat," Flora said. "Shall we give a name to it? Extortion?"

"Call it what you wish."

She smiled, tightly. "Now that we understand each other, what is it you and your people want from me?"

Jay went to the landing and called out. "Manuel Lizárraga! Will you come up, please?"

In a moment the giant was on the landing, anxious. "*Señor?*" He looked hesitantly about. For a man who had just fought bravely in battle he seemed almost frightened by the rich furnishings, the oil paintings on the walls, all so different from his rude jacal in Mex Town.

"*Qué quiere usted, señor?* What do you want of me?"

"I want you to come in and tell Señorita Lamon what it is *la gente* demand."

Manuel's dark eyes rolled. "My English — not so good."

Jay took him by the elbow. "Good enough, *hombre*."

In the darkened office Manuel Lizárraga faced them, hat respectfully in his hands. "*Señorita. Señor.*" He cleared his throat, looked at Jay.

222

"Go ahead, *amigo*. Tell them!"

Awkwardly, painfully, Manuel started. "We — we need more money, sirs. We can not live on the little you pay us." He stopped again, looked at Jay, who nodded.

"We want better places to live, maybe — maybe —" His tongue licked at his white teeth. "Maybe some little *casas* — houses — like we hear the workers have in the mines around the Río de los Palos and the Sierra Piloncillo." As he spoke his voice grew firmer. "We want better conditions in the mines — more *bombas* to keep the water out —"

"Pumps," Jay translated.

"*Sí, señor* — pomps."

"That's ridiculous!" Dineen broke in. "Pumps cost a lot of money, and —"

"We want better *vigas* — timbering — so people are not crushed under rock falls! We want new lift cables, because the old ones are ragged and torn. We want more room for our Dr. Carmody's hospital, and *dinero* for him to buy the medicines he needs."

Dineen was furious. "You can't come in here and —"

"Anything more?" Flora asked crisply, cutting him off.

"One thing more, *señorita*. We are born, we work, we die, and nobody asks God to look down, pity us, help us. We must have a proper church, and a *padre*."

Flora was silent, and Jay could not read her face. Again her fingers, the long delicate fingers ornamented with jeweled rings, tapped the polished surface of the table. After a long pause she spoke, voice firm and her chin slightly lifted.

"I grant you many things have been wrong. But you must know, Señor Lizárraga, that the Lamon interests are in serious financial difficulties. There is just no way we can satisfy such demands. We have heavy cash obligations in the East, and are far behind in scheduled payments to our bankers, mostly because of the operation in Peru that is not yet carrying its share of the load. Add to that the drop in production from the Territory mines, and we — I — will be lucky if I can save the company."

Lizárraga looked at Jay for guidance.

"Then," Jay said, calling what he believed to be a bluff, "the strike must go on. The men will refuse to work under such conditions. They will stop others, if such there are, from replacing them in the diggings; they have the arms to do it. They will stop the pumps, let the mines flood. Mohave City will become a deserted place, with nothing living here but snakes and scorpions. Would your father have risked that?"

She flushed. "Don't push me too far! I am not used to being talked to like this! How dare you?"

"I dare," he said, "because the *mineros* and I both wanted the same thing — to be treated like human beings."

It was too much for Dineen. "Flora, God damn it, don't talk any more to these rascals! Give them an inch and they'll take a mile! If you even *think* of dealing with them, I'll quit. You can run the damned mines yourself, and won't that be nice! In a month the whole place will go to wrack and ruin!" Trembling with rage, he slapped the Colombian hat against his knee; in the quietness of the room it sounded almost like a pistol shot. "And there stands the cause of it all!" He pointed at Jay. "He came in here to stir them up, that's what he did! Until he came —"

Lizárraga, fearing violence to Jay, moved quickly between them, machete poised.

"Emmett, don't talk like that!" Flora's composure was suddenly shattered. "I depended on *you*, at least! We can do it! Between us, we can give them some satisfaction, perhaps, and —"

"Listen!" Jay said. "Listen to me, both of you! I have a plan."

"What plan?" Dineen demanded.

"We know your problems, ma'am. To save the company we must all cooperate. Suppose the miners go back to work, work hard to bring production up to where it was before the troubles — maybe even higher. Let's suppose you give the *mineros* your solemn word to improve their situation — not at once, of course, but gradually, as circumstances permit, making an honest effort to do what they ask — which, in sum, is not unreasonable. What do you think?"

"Flora," Dineen pleaded, "don't be a damned fool! Don't haggle with these rascals! The cards are all in our hand, not theirs!"

She bit her lip. "Be quiet, Emmett! I am thinking."

Dineen pressed hard. "You can't run the place yourself, Flora — you know that!" In an arrogant gesture he tossed the sweat-damp hair away from his forehead. "Maybe it's time for me to state a proposition. If you want me to stay and help you, you'll have to reject all this mealymouthed talk about new lift cables and timbering and little houses. I can get other miners, I know I can — good hardworking Indians that won't give us trouble! You and I, we can run the place to suit ourselves!"

Torn, Flora looked at him, then at Jay. "I — I don't know what to do! If Father — if he only —"

Jay interrupted. "If you need Dineen to stay and help you, ma'am, I can assure you he will do so, regardless of his own thoughts on the matter."

"What does that mean?" Dineen snapped.

Jay reached into the inner pocket of his frayed black coat and brought out the envelope in which he had put Polonius Yount's account of Wagstaff's murder. The envelope was creased and stained, but retained its seal.

Flora stared at the envelope. "Now what is this, pray?"

"This envelope," Jay said, "contains a signed and witnessed statement from someone who saw Mr. Dineen kill the deputy. Dineen and Wagstaff got into an argument over you, ma'am. Mr. Dineen has a volatile temper. He snatched up a Mexican knife from Wagstaff's desk. He and the deputy struggled. Dineen knocked him down, plunged the knife into his back."

The room was silent, the only sound a murmur of voices from the crowd outside. A child laughed, then a low musical note sounded; the *Cocopah* returning from upriver. In his sojourn at Mohave City Jay had learned to distinguish the boats by the whistles.

"It's a damned lie!" Dineen blurted. One hand pulled at his wilted collar. "I don't know anything about it! You can't prove anything!"

"There was a witness," Jay said relentlessly. "Someone saw the whole thing, and is willing to testify in court."

Flora's gaze was unbelieving. "Emmett! You — you didn't!"

"Of course not! Don't you see, Flora — he's only trying to undermine your relationship with me! He's been trying to do that ever since he got here — didn't I always say that?"

Flora's hand trembled as the jeweled fingers worked at the ornamental gold lion on a chain around her slender neck. Under her gaze Dineen looked finally away; black stains showed under the armpits of the white cotton coat.

"I — I see," Flora said finally. Her voice was small, faint. "Now I see." She leaned far back on the great chair, her face an enigma. Fascinated, Jay watched her. *Flawed*, he thought, *but magnificently flawed*. There was much in her he respected. "That is how he died," she said. "Over — over me."

"Flora, for God's sake —"

"So you see," Jay said softly, "you can do what you like with him. He will stay, and I think he will be a help to you as long as you hold that envelope in a safe place."

Hesitantly, Dineen approached the still figure, holding the Colombian hat before him in a gesture Jay had often seen. It was the way the Mexicans had approached their white masters.

"Flora, let's go someplace and talk this over. I'm sure there has been some mistake. I can prove my innocence! If you'll only let me talk to you — explain —"

She waved him away. "Emmett, you are becoming tiresome!" To Jay she said, "You have described a plan as to how we all might work together to save the mines and at the same time better the conditions of the miners."

"Ma'am, I did."

"I assume you speak for the miners."

Manuel Lizárraga interrupted, proudly. "*Sí, señorita* — he is our *jefe!*"

"Then I accept the proposition as stated. If they will go back to work and help me by working hard, then you have my word that I will do everything possible to meet their demands. And I never say something I do not mean, you may trust me on that. It is — something my father taught me." She turned to Emmett Dineen. "You may go now! I have something to say to Dr. Carmody — Mr. Carmody."

Dineen walked unsteadily past Jay, looking down into the woven straw of the hat. At the door he paused.

"Flora?"

"Go, please."

He nodded, slowly closed the door after him.

"Manuel," Jay said, "*por favor, amigo* — go down and tell your people they have won."

228

CHAPTER
THIRTEEN

Flora and Jay Carmody were together a long time in the library, listening to the shouts and cheers and hurrahs dying in the distance as the *mineros* hurried away, probably to arrange *una fiesta grande*. Finally Jay said, "It appears there might be a Fourth of July celebration after all, though some different from the one a year ago."

Flora stared at him, a long and unfathomable look in her steady gray eyes. "You are a remarkable man, Jay Carmody. After all that has happened, after all you have done to me and my father, I want still to call you Jay. May I?"

He was very tired, and his knee hurt. Still he stood, almost respectfully. "Yes. Of course."

"Father always got what he wanted. I always got what I wanted. I suppose we got used to that, we Lamons." She sighed, for a time was silent. Below, the *Cocopah* whistled again, warping into the landing. Flora asked, very suddenly, "Do you love Sarah Iredale?"

Taken aback, he stammered. "I — I — well, I guess so! Anyway, I intend to ask for her hand as soon as I can. Yes, of course I love her! Sarah is a fine woman!"

Flora nodded, her face bleak. "I envy her. I — I always envied her. I knew Sarah was a fine woman — better than me, certainly. Perhaps I hated her, too, for that."

For a long time she was again silent, Flora staring at her jeweled fingers, Jay not knowing what to say. His knee ached abominably; he shifted his position.

"What are your plans, then?"

He hadn't thought much beyond the moment. "Sarah and I — if she'll have me, that is — we'll go down on the *Cocopah* and be married in Yuma."

"What will Mohave City, what will the mines and the mill and the people do without a doctor?"

He almost blurted out that they never had a doctor, not a real one, anyway. But the pride remained. He hadn't done at all badly.

"Well, there's a final request I'd like to make of you, ma'am."

"Flora! Please, Jay — Flora!"

"As you please — Flora. Anyway, what I was going to say — your father will need a real doctor. For now old María and Concepción and Concha can take care of the patients in the hospital. They're capable women, good nurses, and I've taught them what I know about medicine. But your father — and the town — must have a proper physician. I — I hope you will place another notice in the *Call*." He smiled, wryly. "This time, examine the doctor's qualifications more closely."

She did not smile. "Beyond Yuma, then — what?"

He straightened, wincing at his bad leg. "Somehow I'm going back to the San Francisco College of

230

Homeopathic Medicine and Surgery, this time as a real student. There's nothing I want more to be, I've found, than a physician. We won't have much money, but somehow we'll manage, Sarah and I."

Flora nodded, said nothing more. When he fidgeted, she rose, preceded him down the stairs. On the porch outside stood the man in the well-cut coat, the man Jay had once mistaken for Tucker Stiles the day the stranger got off the *Cocopah* looking for a place to stay. He was smoking a stogie; when he saw Flora he threw the cigar away and took off his round-crowned hat.

"Miss Flora Lamon?"

"Yes?"

The visitor waved toward the town. "Been fireworks here today, ma'am! Lots of excitement." He held up the hat, pointing to a neat hole in the crown. "Took a shot in this expensive *sombrero* this morning when I wasn't fast enough getting out of the way!"

"You wanted to talk to me, sir?"

The bearded man bowed. "I'm George P. Willetts, ma'am — member of the Arizona Legislature."

Jay's mouth felt dry and cottony. Was this the end of his great adventure? Was Mr. Willetts looking for him on a criminal charge — impersonating a doctor, or more likely, leader of an insurrection?

"Used to know your father, ma'am," Willetts went on. "He and I were partners in the Sidewinder diggings in Sonora a long time ago. We were both pups. Well —" The old man broke off, cleared his throat. "Anyway, Governor Safford has been concerned about conditions in the Territory mines, particularly conditions in the

Lamon mines, not to put too fine a point on it. He appointed me a committee of one to come down here and look into charges that the Mexicans were something real close to slaves in your pa's mines. So if it's all right with you, ma'am, I'd like to talk to old Andy."

Flora looked at him coolly. "I'm afraid that's impossible. My father has had a sudden fit of apoplexy, and is even now lying helpless in his bed. You can, if you like, speak with me, Mr. Willetts, about the Lamon mines. But I can assure you that improvements are being made immediately. I am now running the mines myself." She looked at Jay. "Dr. Carmody here has been — has been very instrumental in bringing about beneficial changes."

Willetts looked shrewdly at Jay, stroked his beard. "Dr. Carmody, sir! Heard a lot about you already. As you no doubt know, I've been here for several days, sniffing around here and there, talking to people."

With the mill silent, from the Lamon veranda they could hear the sound of revelry from Mex Town — a tootling fife, the bray of a battered cornet. A hoarded rocket of some sort soared into the air, exploded, and left a streamer of pale smoke drifting across the river. The rain had gone, and Mohave City baked again in the July sun.

"I'd say that the way this whole thing was managed is something quite odd," Mr. Willetts mused, staring at the wind-whipped smoke. "A person could call it a revolution, I suppose, something peaceful Arizona citizens usually leave to the hotheads in Sonora and

Chihuahua." He ran thumb and finger around the brim of his hat, thoughtfully. "You say your pa is ill, ma'am?"

Jay was about to confirm Flora's statement, to say he had been Andrew Lamon's personal physician. The words stuck in his throat. He was not a physician; word of his unmasking must have spread.

"I have already told you that, sir. If you wish, you may come in and discuss matters with me. I speak now for my father." When Mr. Willetts looked doubtful, Flora's chin raised. "Do you doubt me, sir?"

Mr. Willetts was a successful politician. "No, ma'am, I do not. It is just that such a beautiful lady —"

"You will find me competent to answer any questions you may wish to ask."

"I thank you, ma'am, and will take advantage of your offer to complete my report to Governor Safford. But now I see you are weary, and I do not wish to take advantage of your grief. Right now, perhaps I'd better speak to Dr. Carmody here, and return later to take testimony from you."

Flora nodded, her face drawn and pale. "That would be best, I believe." For a moment her composure weakened; to Jay she looked extraordinarily like a little girl who has been hurt by an insensitive world.

"Flora —" he said.

She smiled a tight smile, and gave him her hand. "Jay, goodbye. Now I must see to Father."

"Goodbye, Flora," he murmured. "And — good luck, always."

Limping down the steps, Jay escorted Mr. Willetts along the graveled road toward town.

"You're an extraordinary man, Dr. Carmody," Mr. Willetts remarked. "I've learned a great deal about you since I've been in Mohave City. It seems that you —"

"Excuse me!" Jay blurted. In the distance he saw her — Sarah Iredale, a small figure waiting at the edge of town near old Don Jaime's jacal. "I — I have an appointment! There is someone I — I —" Seeing Sarah, he never wanted so much in his life to be with anyone, to throw his arms about her, to kiss her and draw her tightly to him. Abandoning Mr. Willetts he limped toward her, faster and faster, wanting to share with her, to tell her everything.

"Sarah!" he called. "I'm coming!"

Monk Griffin donated his beer to the *fiesta*. That night Mex Town vibrated with merriment and goodwill. Luke Hodge, Mrs. Hodge watching warily, danced the fandango with Concepción Macías. Homer Fox, the blacksmith, played a homemade banjo in concert with the Mexican guitars. Mr. Willetts attended the celebration, sitting in a chair clapping his hands while the Mexican belles flashed around the floor in a kaleidoscope of color that brightened the drab room where Jay Carmody and Tucker Stiles had been sentenced, once, to be hanged. Jay and Sarah were honored guests — the heart and center of the *gran baile*.

Mr. Willetts had decided that results were really the thing. "I trust Miss Lamon to change things for the better," he told Jay. "It appears Deputy Wagstaff was killed by a person or persons unknown, and it's not likely anyone will ever find out who did it. I'll see that another deputy is sent out — a fair and reasonable man, one not on the payroll of the Lamons — and of course I'll keep an eye on things here and see how it goes. But in the meantime, let's enjoy ourselves, eh?"

Dancing with Sarah in a far corner of the room, Jay put a cheek close to hers in a display of intimacy. No one seemed to notice, or care. She pressed back. "Jay, I'm so happy for you, and for them." She nodded toward the Mexicans. "And — for me, too."

Seeing the pigtailed Ah Sing grinning moonfaced at him, Jay blushed, excused himself. Walking across the room to where Jorge Macías was plucking an exotic-looking Mexican instrument, a huge guitar-looking box that gave a thunderous beat to the music, Jay touched his sleeve. "*Jorge, hombre* —"

Jorge paused in his plucking. "*Señor?*"

"I never thought to thank you."

Jorge looked puzzled, wiped a sweating brow. "Thank me? *Porqué, señor?*"

"That night — the time you came to the jail, a year ago, when my friend and I were sentenced to hang."

"*Sí, señor.* We found, my brother and I, that it was to be *un chiste*, a kind of joke. We thought it not right for the Lamon people to do that to a man, any man — one of God's creatures, like *la gente*. I wanted to tell you not to be afraid, it was only a bad joke, but someone shot at me and I ran." With the back of a hand he hit himself smartly on the forehead. "*Ay, que cobarde!* What a coward I was then!"

"No," Jay said. "You were a brave man, a decent man. And again I thank you." He embraced Jorge, and for some reason, this time he did not feel foolish. It was, he decided reluctantly, a nice thing to do. "*Gracias, amigo.*"

Later, Rubén Macías made a speech.

"Don Diego, *amigo*, you came to help us when no one else would. You bound up our wounds, found us guns to fight with, gave us of your courage. Now we lift up our heads and are proud men again, no longer slaves. We are *mineros* who work hard — not because we are driven to it but because we want to help Señorita Lamon get the mines going again."

There was a cheer that lasted till Rubén raised a big hand.

"And now — does a piece of paper make a doctor? No! A doctor is a doctor! Never was there a better one than Don Diego, our own *señor doctor!* Someday, we know, he will come back to us!"

Cries of acclaim split the hot night. "*Viva el nuestro doctor! Viva el señor doctor, el gran maestro! Viva! Viva!*"

Jay was embarrassed as they tugged at his sleeve, tried to kiss his hand, pushed and shoved and struggled just to be near him. Once he looked toward Sarah Iredale, helplessly. Though her eyes were bright with tears, she was smiling, and raised a hand to wave at him.

Epilogue

When Jay and Sarah and old Major Iredale left on the *Cocopah* a throng of townspeople, Mexicans, and Indians jammed the wharf. They all brought gifts. Homer Fox gave Sarah a heavy gold chain, handmade. The Hodges brought a gilt-framed horsehair picture — "from my old home in Cairo, Illinois," the weeping Mrs. Hodge said — and Monk Griffin gave Jay a bottle of Scotch whiskey and Sarah a bottle of perfume "from a gal I onct knew." The Mexican gifts were things the *mineros* and their families had made, or precious possessions: framed crayon scenes, bags of the sugar candy called *panoche*, religious medals and icons. There was a gorgeous handmade lace-ruffled shirt with lace collar and cuffs — "to wear at your wedding, *señor*" — and a beautiful lace shawl for Sarah. Jay and his intended tried to refuse, but there was no way; the gifts were for the *jefe* and his *novia*, his sweetheart.

"Same rate!" Captain Thorne grinned when Jay tried to pay their passage to Yuma. "You go free, Doc!"

"But — the major and Miss Sarah —"

"Family, ain't they? We carry the whole family on one ticket!"

As they splashed downstream to a chorus of tearful farewells Sarah and Jay remained on the boiler deck, eyes misty. Major Iredale stood in the bows of the vessel, firm in the conviction the *Cocopah* was chasing a Union ironclad across Mobile Bay. The sun shone bright, and for a moment Jay caught a golden blink in an upper room of the Lamon mansion, high on the hill in its frame of green. Flora, at her father's brass telescope in the library? He chose to think so, and waved.

Sarah moved closer, hand on his arm. "Goodbye to Mohave City."

She had misinterpreted his gesture, but Jay chose not to explain.

He nodded. "Goodbye — to all that."

Captain Thorne, leaving the wheel to the mate, opened the pilothouse door and handed Jay an envelope. "Almost forgot! She said to give it to you when we were well under way."

"She?"

Thorne grinned, handed him also a small but heavy canvas sack. "This too." He went forward, hands jammed in his pockets, whistling.

Jay stared at the envelope, addressed in a feminine hand. Opening it, he smelled familiar perfume:

Dear Jay —

I am sending to the *Cocopah*, with my best wishes, funds to contribute to the education of a doctor. Money is scarce right now, but I have gone over our books and we can surely spare this much

238

for a good cause. Maybe someday you will return and see for yourself how the mines have changed. Until then —

Flora Lamon

"What is it?" Sarah asked.

He showed her the note.

"She is an unusual lady," Sarah said softly. "In a way, I admired her."

"She admired you also."

He undid the leather thong securing the bag. Incredulous, they both stared. The bag contained several pounds of the Lamon "mint drops," pure and soft, sticking together.

"My goodness!" Sarah breathed. "There must be a thousand dollars' worth!"

Jay took one out and looked at it. Gold, pure gold — with Andrew Lamon's mark on it, as Lamon's mark had once been on everything and every person in Mohave City. What men would do for this yellow stuff! Cheat, lie, betray, even kill! "Over a thousand," he agreed. Well, he would put it to good use. As for coming back to Mohave City someday — who knew?

When Sarah went below to rest, Jay remained at the rail. White and foamy, the *Cocopah*'s wake surged behind the vessel. All that now remained of Mohave City was a pillar of smoke marking the sprawling mill that was again firing up. Reaching into a coat pocket, he took out the small notebook in which he had kept an accounting of his enemies. Idly he wondered what Tuck Stiles would have thought of the way things turned out.

Deciding it made no difference now, he drew back his arm and threw the notebook in a high arc over the rail. For a long time it bobbed in the *Cocopah*'s wake, white pages fluttering. Then it disappeared from view.

Satisfied, Jay picked up the bag of mint drops and went below to join Sarah.